D1010993

INVASION OF THE LIVING TED

ALSO BY BARRY HUTCHISON

Night of the Living Ted
Revenge of the Living Ted

INVASION OF THE LIVING TED

BARRY HUTCHISON ILLUSTRATED BY LEE COSGROVE

Delacorte Press

Text copyright © 2019 by Barry Hutchison
Cover and interior illustrations copyright © 2019 by Lee Cosgrove

Visit us on the Web! rhcbooks.com

Educators and librarians, for a variety of teaching tools, visit us at RHTeachersLibrarians.com

Library of Congress Cataloging-in-Publication Data is available upon request.
ISBN 978-0-593-17432-6 (hc) — ISBN 978-0-593-17433-3 (ebook)

Printed in the United States of America
10 9 8 7 6 5 4 3 2 1
First American Edition

For everyone at Inverlochy Primary School
—B.H.

For Alex and Sophia—*Dum spiro spero*
—L.C.

INVASION OF THE LIVING TED

"Yes, yes, Agent Strong, we get it. It's very important that we not tell anyone about the teddy bears, or what happened on the hillside," said Lisa Marie, interrupting the man in the dark suit and sunglasses.

Lisa Marie sat on one side of a narrow desk in the back of a cramped van, holding the gaze of the man sitting on the other side.

Vernon, her stepbrother, sat squashed in the narrow space beside her, making little panicky yelps whenever Lisa Marie said anything that might make the man angry. Agent Strong was a large man. Very large, in fact. So large that his head almost touched the low roof of the van, forcing him to duck a little.

"Honestly, you're treating us like children," said Lisa Marie. "I mean, obviously we *are* children, but we're not idiots. You don't have to keep asking us the same questions over and over. We've already told you everything."

Vernon squeaked like a frightened mouse. "Lisa Marie, what are you doing?" he whimpered, forcing a smile that showed every single one of his teeth. "Let the scary gentleman speak." He shook his head. "I mean *nice* gentleman. Nice gentleman . . ."

"We answered your questions and signed all your forms yesterday," Lisa Marie continued, ignoring her stepbrother. "And the day before that. You don't need to—"

She and Vernon both grabbed the edge of the desk and hung on as the van turned a corner. A small pile of paperwork started sliding across the desktop, then stopped when Agent Strong brought his fist down on it with a *bang*.

They all waited until the swinging movement had stopped. Then Lisa Marie picked up right where she had left off.

"—go through it all over again. We're not going to tell anyone about the teddies coming to life, or Ursine Kodiak's inventions, or any of the other stuff. We understand the consequences. If we do, then you'll throw us and our parents in prison. You've gone to great pains to make that *extremely* clear."

And he had. When Strong and the other government agents had come to the house after the latest teddy bear incident, he'd made them watch a slideshow about the prison they'd be sent to. He'd even pointed out some of the "fun highlights," which included a strict seven p.m. bedtime, rats in the kitchen and a bucket in the corner for pooping in.

Dad had made a joke about it, saying it sounded like the camp they'd gone to last summer. Nobody laughed. But then, Dad had joked pretty much nonstop since the government agents had brought Lisa Marie and Vernon home, following their battle with the teddies. He and Mom hadn't believed any of it at first, but then Bearvis had started speaking and they'd had no choice but to accept the truth.

Joking was Dad's way of dealing with it, Lisa Marie knew. She just wished his jokes were actually funny.

"Look, kids, I get it. I do," said Agent Strong, holding up his hands in what was supposed to be a friendly gesture. "But this is important. National-security-level important. Maybe world security."

The agent clasped his hands together and leaned closer. "If word gets out that someone tried to take over this town with an army of teddy bears, and that very same someone is still at large, there will be mass panic."

"If you mean Ursine Kodiak," said Lisa Marie, "I already told you—he wasn't responsible. I mean, he was to begin with, but then Grizz took over. Ursine helped us in the end. Kind of. Well, a bit."

"Either way," said Agent Strong. "Mass panic."

"Will there be, though?" asked Vernon.

Agent Strong lowered his sunglasses just a fraction and peered over the top with his steel-blue eyes. Vernon almost fell off his seat in alarm.

"I mean, sure, yes, you're right—mass panic," Vernon agreed. He swallowed and tried to smile again. It didn't go well. "But, um, I mean, will people . . . ? You know? About the . . . ? I'm not sure . . . Do you think . . . ?"

Lisa Marie put a hand on Vernon's arm. He immediately stopped talking and exhaled with relief.

"What my brother is trying to ask is: Would people believe it even if we *did* tell them?" she said. "Which we won't," she added quickly. "The only witnesses were us and a few other kids, and they just thought the bears were high-tech robots. Who's going to believe us if we say an army of evil teddy bears came to life?"

"Which, again, we won't," Vernon added.

Agent Strong regarded them both for a while, and then shrugged. "People will believe anything, if you try hard enough."

There was a screech of brakes. Agent Strong's paperwork went shooting off the desk and landed in his lap. He sighed, picked it up, then slammed it back on the desk.

"Interview terminated," he said. "You may go."

Vernon emitted a nervous laugh and jumped to his feet. His head hit the roof with a *thonk*, but he was too excited to be leaving to care.

"What? No," Lisa Marie argued. "You said you'd tell us where Bearvis and the other teddies are. The Duds. They helped us save this town. They're not like the other bears—they're on our side. What have you done with them?"

Agent Strong pushed his sunglasses back up so they were hiding his eyes.

"They are . . . helping us with our enquiries, miss," he said. Lisa Marie hated it when he called her "miss." Somehow he managed to make it sound like an insult. "Their whereabouts must remain a secret for now, in the interest—"

"Of national security. We get it," said Lisa Marie. She placed both arms on the desk and leaned forward. She could see herself reflected in Strong's dark glasses and didn't think she'd ever seen herself look so angry. "But I swear, if you've hurt those bears, you're going to have me to answer to."

Her eyes narrowed. "You might not think that's very scary, coming from a nine-year-old girl, but trust me, it is."

Agent Strong said nothing for a long time, then gestured to the door behind the children. "You're going to be late for school."

"If we *are* late, it'll be thanks to you," said Lisa Marie crossly. Behind her, Vernon slid open the door, letting early-morning sunlight flood in.

Lisa Marie shot Agent Strong a last stern look;

then she and Vernon both jumped out of the van and landed with a *tha-thack* on the road.

Lisa Marie turned around. Her face softened as her anger was replaced by concern. "If you see Bearvis, will you tell him I said hi?" she asked.

Agent Strong said nothing for a moment, then gestured with one of his giant hands. "Please close the door," he said. "Oh, and I'll be waiting for you after school. We have a few more questions to ask about this 'Grizz' character."

Lisa Marie's anger came rushing back. "Great! We can't *wait*," she snapped. Then she slammed the door as hard as she could. The van sped away in a cloud of exhaust fumes, the word "PIZZA" printed on the side in large black letters.

"Thanks for the lift!" Vernon called after the van. "See you soon . . . Uncle Italy."

Lisa Marie frowned up at him. *"What?"*

"Cover story," Vernon whispered. "If anyone asks why we got a lift to school in a pizza van, we'll say it was our uncle."

"Yes, I get that bit," said Lisa Marie. "But *Uncle Italy?*"

Vernon blushed slightly. "It was the only Italian name I could think of."

Lisa Marie rolled her eyes. "Genius," she said. She shot another glance toward the van. "It's not fair."

"Yeah," Vernon agreed. "Can't believe the weekend's over already. School is so unfair."

"Not *school*! Agent Strong. It's not fair he can hold on to Bearvis and the Duds and keep pulling us in for questioning."

Vernon shrugged. "Better that than having to deal with Grizz and his evil teddies, though," he said. He chewed his lip for a moment. "You think they're gone? For good this time, I mean?"

"I hope so," said Lisa Marie. "But best to stay alert, just in case."

The school bell rang, calling the children to class.

"Still, at least the day's not a total disaster," she said, brightening. "We've got a math test this afternoon! Don't you just love Mondays?"

Vernon groaned. "Yay, Mondays!" he said miserably. Then he trudged through the school gates after his stepsister, dragging his feet.

Although Lisa Marie and Vernon's weekend had been pretty bad, it was nothing compared to Ursine Kodiak's.

He hadn't washed. He hadn't slept. He hadn't eaten. Well, unless you counted the cashew he'd found in his straggly beard in the early hours of Sunday morning, which he'd gobbled down before the monster living inside his head could stop him.

His back ached, his feet hurt and his eyes were dry and itchy. His fingers were sore from twiddling and fiddling with wires, tapping keys, twisting screws, and a million and one other things he'd had to do to get the machine up and running.

But now, at last, it was almost done.

"What's taking so long?" demanded the voice inside Ursine's head. He knew it was coming from inside his head, and yet he heard the words as if they had been growled in his ear.

The voice belonged to a teddy bear. At least, that's what it had started out as. Grizz had been a Halloween bear built by Vernon, who had come to life and led an army of ghost bears, vampire bears, witch bears and werewolf bears in an attempt to take over the town.

Lisa Marie and Vernon had put a stop to that, but unbeknown to them, Ursine Kodiak had been so fascinated by Grizz that he'd created an artificial intelligence—a computer brain—that was an exact replica of the original Grizz.

Unfortunately for Ursine, he had underestimated quite how wicked and cunning Grizz was. The AI bear had inserted a control chip into Ursine's head and installed himself on it. Now not only could he boss Ursine around, he could control him too.

Like at this very moment, for example, when Grizz thought Ursine wasn't working quite hard enough.

THWACK!

Ursine slapped himself across the face, tugged on an ear, then flicked his nose.

"Ow! Stop that!" he protested.

His foot shot up, kicking him on the bottom.

"Stop it!"

"Then hurry up!" Grizz growled. "What's taking you so long?"

Ursine sighed and gestured around. When the police and the army had turned up at his head-quarters, he'd been forced to flee to one of his old workshops in London. It had been built in an abandoned Underground station. It was dark and damp and now thick with dust. All the equipment rattled whenever trains passed along the neigh-bouring tracks. Which was often.

Junk and abandoned inventions lay scattered around the place, piled up in corners, or stacked

against walls. Taking over the world had been an ambition of Ursine's for as long as he could remember, and before he'd settled on his "evil teddy bear" theme, he'd built freeze rays, weather-control devices, hypnosis watches, and even a shrinking ray. They had all worked fine, but none of his schemes had felt quite right until the bear army.

And look where that had gotten him.

"I'm working as hard as I can," he explained. "But the equipment here is very basic. I don't have an omemoscope, half the crimplets are rusted, and one of the handles has come off the borewonger."

"I have no idea what you're even saying to me right now," Grizz said, then he made Ursine slap himself in the face again. "Stop making up words and speak English."

Ursine stamped his foot. It was a small foot, which was surprising given that the rest of him was so big and bulky. "Will you *please* stop that?" he asked. "What I'm trying to say is that I think I've done rather well, considering the limitations. I've almost finished the machine."

He could feel Grizz's excitement vibrating the chip inside his head.

"And it'll do what I want?"

"It will," Ursine confirmed.

"*Exactly* what I want?"

"Yes! It'll do exactly what you told me to make it do," Ursine said. He puffed up his chest, just a little. "I'm rather proud of it, actually. It's an incredibly clever blend of advanced science and dark magic. I don't want to boast—"

"So don't!" Grizz said.

Ursine tugged on his beard and bit his tongue.

"Ow!" he yelped. "Thtop that!"

"What do you still have to do?" Grizz demanded.

Ursine opened his mouth to reply, then braced himself against one of the cracked-tile walls as a train thundered past in an adjacent tunnel. Dust cascaded from the ceiling. Rats squeaked in the shadows. The other handle fell off the borewonger.

Once everything had settled down, Ursine continued.

"I need to amalgamate the central console with the fiber-optic transmission unit," he said.

Thwack.

"English!"

Ursine let out a sob, then pointed to two pieces of equipment that sat side by side on a cluttered workbench. "I need to stick that bit to that bit," he said.

"Better," growled Grizz. "And remember, I can see right into your brain from here, so I'll know if you try any funny stuff. Mess up my plans, and I'll mess up your head. Got it?"

"Got it," said Ursine.

"Good. Then hop to it."

Ursine didn't so much hop as shuffle across to the workbench. He yawned, his mouth appearing like a wide hole in the middle of his bushy beard.

"Right. Yes. I will," he said, his voice soft and slurred. "I wonder if I might . . . just . . . have a . . ."

His head fell forward and thunked on to the workbench. A moment later, he began to snore.

"Wake up!" Grizz instructed. "Wake up, before . . ."

Inside Ursine's head, Grizz felt the sleepy darkness approaching. "Stupid meatbag," he spat, and then the darkness closed around him, the control chip entered Rest Mode, and he too fell fast asleep.

Lisa Marie liked Mondays. Every Monday, because she was a genius at math, she got to spend the day in Vernon's class doing some higher-level lessons.

She'd had to work hard to convince the teachers it was a good idea, but eventually they'd agreed to a trial day.

And when she'd pointed out a mistake in the teacher's long division on that first morning, and scored higher than everyone else on the afternoon test, Lisa Marie knew she was there to stay.

Sure enough, she'd been back to the class every week since, and Monday had quickly become her favorite day of the week. Lisa Marie always sat at the spare desk at the front of the class and enjoyed not having the distraction of the older children chatting around her—it was easier to concentrate.

Today, though, she was having trouble keeping her mind on her work. She found herself staring out the classroom window, only half listening to the teacher, Miss Watson.

Miss Watson was one of only two downsides to higher-level math. The teacher shouted a lot, and had never really forgiven Lisa Marie for correcting her long division.

Miss Watson stood at the head of the class now, trying to remember how the interactive whiteboard worked. Lisa Marie could've fixed it for her, but she didn't feel like lending a hand today. She was too worried about Bearvis, the Elvis bear who'd helped her and Vernon defeat Grizz and his teddy bear army—twice! Wherever the government had taken Bearvis, she hoped they were taking good care of him.

An eraser boinged off the back of her head, closely followed by the sound of someone sniggering. Lisa Marie sighed. That was the other downside of being in Vernon's class.

"Drake, do you mind?" Lisa Marie asked, turning and glaring at the biggest boy in the room. He was sitting next to Vernon, who stared back at Lisa Marie in horror, silently shaking his head at her.

Everyone in school was afraid of Drake, except Lisa Marie. It was hard to be scared of someone once you'd seen them transformed into a cute little teddy with a pink bow on their head.

Lisa Marie bent and picked up the eraser from where it had landed on the floor. At the front of the class, Miss Watson sensed some mischief going on.

"Is something the matter?" the teacher demanded.

"Drake threw his eraser at me," said Lisa Marie.

"What? No I didn't!" Drake snapped. He elbowed Vernon in the ribs. "Did I, Vern?"

Vernon's mouth flapped open and closed. "Well . . . I mean . . ."

"See?" said Drake. "I didn't do it."

Lisa Marie held up the eraser for everyone to see. All eyes were on her now, watching with interest. "So this isn't yours?"

Drake grinned and leaned back in his chair. "Nope."

"Then why does it say *Drake's eraser—hands off* on it?"

Drake's smile fell away. "Anyone could've written that," he said.

Miss Watson rolled her eyes. "I think I've heard quite enough," she said. "Really, Drake. When are you ever going to learn?" She picked up a pen and made a note on the whiteboard. To her obvious relief, it worked. "There. *Detention for Drake*," she said, indicating where she'd written the words.

Lisa Marie raised a hand.

"Yes?" said Miss Watson.

"That says *detetion*," Lisa Marie pointed out.

Miss Watson looked back at the board and tutted. "So it does." She clicked the mouse on the computer attached to the whiteboard. Nothing happened. She tried again. "How do I get rid of it?" she asked the class.

Lisa Marie raised her hand.

"Yes?"

"You can't, miss," Lisa Marie told her. "You've written it in Sharpie."

Miss Watson looked down at the pen in her hand, then over to the digital pens specially designed to use with the whiteboard. Her face went almost as pale as the board itself.

"Oh, not again," she whispered, hurrying toward the door in a panic. "I'm just going to find Mr. Bryant. Carry on from where we left off yesterday."

Lisa Marie raised her hand to point out that yesterday was Sunday, but Miss Watson had already raced out of the room to get the custodian.

"Three, two, one . . . ," Lisa Marie whispered.

Another eraser bounced off the back of her head.

Behind her, Drake and a few of the other boys cackled with laughter. She hoped Vernon wasn't one of them. Although he'd stood up to Drake once before, her stepbrother was unlikely to do it now, with the other boys around.

Lisa Marie decided to ignore the eraser. She crossed her arms on the desk and slid down so her chin was resting on them. From there, she had a clear view through the window to the playground beyond. The rain had started shortly after school had begun, and the world was now drab and gray.

She knew exactly how it felt.

As she stared outside, the kindergartners passed the window. They were all dressed in raincoats and boots, and they laughed and giggled as they jumped from puddle to puddle.

"Hey, isn't that your class out there, Lisa Marie?" Drake jeered, drawing more laughter from the boys. "They look about your age."

Lisa Marie turned in her seat. "I was going to say they look about your intellectual age," she said. "But I don't want to insult them."

Drake's brow furrowed slowly. "What? Is that an insult?" He looked at Vernon. "Was that an insult?"

"I don't know," lied Vernon. He caught Lisa Marie's eyes and smirked, just a little.

"It better not have been," Drake warned. "Or I'll—"

Whatever he was going to do was cut off by a sudden sharp squeal from outside.

"Teddy! Teddy!"

Lisa Marie sat bolt upright, adrenaline surging through her. No. No, it couldn't be. They'd taken care of the teddies this time, hadn't they? They'd stopped them.

"Help! Help! Teddy! Teddy!" the child outside screamed.

Lisa Marie jumped to her feet, sending her chair clattering to the floor. What if the teddy army was back? She set off running toward the classroom door, determined to find out for sure . . .

And collided with Miss Watson.

"Lisa Marie? Where on earth are you going?"

"Aargh! Get out of the way, you . . . *silly woman!*" Lisa Marie cried. She regretted it immediately. She'd never been rude to a teacher before, and this was probably one of the rudest things a pupil had ever said to Miss Watson.

"Teddy! Teddy! Help!"

There was no time to waste on apologizing. While Miss Watson reeled in shock, Lisa Marie ducked under her arm, raced past Mr. Bryant, skidded round the corner and clattered out through the school doors.

"Hey, leave those kids alone!" she cried, bounding into the playground with her fists raised. "I've beaten you before, I'll beat you . . ." Lisa Marie's voice trailed away as she realized her mistake.

The kindergarten class and their teacher were staring at her in surprise from beneath their jacket hoods. One girl was hopping from foot to foot, pointing at her teddy bear, which had fallen in the biggest, dirtiest puddle in the playground.

"Help my teddy! Miss! Miss! Help my teddy!"

"Don't worry, Alice," the teacher said, stooping to rescue the soft toy. "We'll hang it up to dry in the classroom."

The other children all went back to splashing,

leaving Lisa Marie standing on her own in the rain. She blushed, just a little, then turned and ran back inside before the kindergarten teacher could ask any questions.

By the time she got back to class, Lisa Marie's cheeks were burning with embarrassment. She passed the custodian just as he was leaving, an ink-stained rag in his hand and a fed-up expression on his face.

As she sat down in her seat, she could feel Miss Watson's eyes boring into her. Then the teacher turned and finished writing something on the board.

"*Detention*," Miss Watson read. *"Lisa Marie."*

"What? But—" Lisa Marie began to protest, but she stopped. It was, she supposed, only right. She *had* called Miss Watson a "silly woman." What did she expect?

"Okay, miss," Lisa Marie said. "But you've used Sharpie again."

Miss Watson's eyes crept down to the pen in her hand. She whispered something under her breath, then hurried to the door. "Uh, yoo-hoo! Mr. Bryant?" she called, chasing the custodian down the corridor. "I wonder if I might have another quick word . . . ?"

It was strange being in school after all the other pupils had left. Normally, the corridors were full of noise, no matter what time of day it was.

Now they were still and silent.

Well, almost.

"Ugh. I can't believe we've got to tidy up the stupid kindergarten room," Drake groaned, his big feet slapping along the corridor behind Lisa Marie. "How is that fair?"

"They have finger paints and tricycles. You should love it," said Lisa Marie.

She had to agree, though, that it was a particularly nasty punishment. She'd been hoping to spend her half hour of detention writing an essay, or doing some math. She loved that stuff.

She was less fond of putting away toys and tidying up the mess left by a large group of four- and five-year-olds.

She wasn't exactly relishing the company either. She liked that word. *Relishing.* It meant "greatly enjoying," and was a word she often liked to use.

She relished science lessons. She relished math tests. She did not relish the thought of being stuck with Drake for thirty minutes. Even worse, she knew she'd be left to do all the work while he lounged around doing nothing.

Ugh. Boys.

"Hey, wait for me!"

Lisa Marie and Drake both turned to see Vernon hurrying along the corridor.

"What are you doing here?" Lisa Marie asked.

Vernon shrugged. "I, uh, told Miss Watson that I swapped her pens around. She thinks it's my fault she keeps drawing on the whiteboard in Sharpie."

"You swapped her pens? Nice!" cackled Drake. He gave Vernon a high five. "Why didn't I think of that? And then owning up to it right to her face. Wicked!"

Lisa Marie frowned at her brother, confused. There was no way he could've switched the teacher's pens. It didn't make sense.

Vernon smiled awkwardly and lowered his voice to a whisper. "Well, I couldn't very well leave you stuck with you-know-who, could I?"

Lisa Marie gave a little nod and returned Vernon's smile. She wanted to give him a hug, but she knew he'd never stand for that sort of thing. Especially in front of Drake.

Boys.

"Right, then," said Lisa Marie as they arrived at the kindergarten classroom. She paused with her hand on the door handle. "Let's see what sort of mess they've left for us."

She opened the door. The first thing she saw was the teddy bear. It was grabbing a thin rope that ran from one side of the classroom to the other, clinging to it with both paws, its glassy black eyes staring at Lisa Marie from just a few yards away.

"Got you!" cried Lisa Marie. She ran toward the bear, swung her foot, and kicked it as hard as she could. The bear flew through the air, splatted against one of the paintings on the wall, then slid slowly to the floor, leaving a wet smear of paint in its wake.

It was only then that Lisa Marie noticed the clothespins attached to the rope where the bear's paws had been. It was the teddy that had fallen in the puddle earlier. The teacher had hung it up to dry.

"Bit of an overreaction," said Vernon. Lisa Marie blushed and flashed him an embarrassed smile.

"Nah, don't listen to him!" Drake snorted. "I like your style, kid. Let's trash this place!"

"Uh, I think we're too late for that," said Vernon. He gestured around the room. Abandoned toys, half-finished artwork and around six good shovelfuls of sand lay scattered all over the floor.

There was a small kitchen in the corner, where the children sometimes did baking, and they'd clearly been busy today, judging by the number of dirty bowls, plates and wooden spoons, and the sticky finger marks that covered almost every surface.

"What happened in here?" Vernon wondered.

"Thirty children," said Lisa Marie. "All aged four or five."

She crossed to where the teddy bear had landed and picked it up carefully by one paw. It looked at her slightly accusingly, she thought, although she could hardly blame it for that.

"Sorry," she whispered, pinning it back onto the line. "False alarm."

She wiped her hands on her school skirt and turned back to the boys. "Okay, let's start by putting away all the—"

Tri-tring.

Lisa Marie watched in silence as Drake weaved across the classroom on a tiny tricycle, hunched over so his knees were up by his ears. He laughed as he swerved around a couple of desks, then collided with a large plastic tub, knocking it over and spilling Lego all over the floor.

"You were right," Drake said, grinning up at Lisa Marie. "This classroom is awesome!"

Lisa Marie rolled her eyes. This was getting them nowhere.

"Vernon, put those boxes in the toy cupboard," she instructed.

Vernon didn't bother to argue. He knew that tone of voice—Lisa Marie was on a mission. He picked up a couple of plastic tubs filled with toy cars and modeling clay and looked around.

"Which one's the toy cupboard?" he asked.

Lisa Marie pointed to a door behind him. "The one with *toys* written on it."

"Ah! Gotcha," said Vernon. He picked his way through the pile of Lego, stopped to let Drake go speeding past him, pedalling madly, then wrestled the door to the toy cupboard open with his elbow.

"Right," he said, then screamed and dropped his boxes as dozens of teddy bears rained down on top of him, knocking him to the floor.

"Vernon!" Lisa Marie cried as her stepbrother disappeared under the pile of bears, sending toy cars flying in all directions.

She raced over and kicked away two of the bears, then noticed that the only thing in the pile that was actually moving was Vernon.

"Aargh! They've got me! They've got me! Save me, Lisa Marie! Help!"

"It's fine. They're just normal teddies," Lisa Marie told him, picking a couple up and tossing them over her shoulder. "Now who's overreacting?"

Vernon was too terrified to listen. Drake stopped pedaling and reversed up to Lisa Marie's side. They both watched Vernon wrestling with a particularly sweet-looking teddy in a red-and-white cheerleader's outfit.

"Seriously," Drake snorted after a while. "What is it with you two and teddy bears?"

Ursine Kodiak awoke with a start, then a scream, then a slap to the face from his left hand.

"What kept you?" demanded Grizz. "I've been awake for ages."

This was not strictly true. Grizz had come back online just a few moments before, when Ursine's brain had started to rise from its exhausted slumber. But there was no way Grizz was telling *him* that.

"Sorry. Sorry," whimpered Ursine. "I was just so tired."

"Don't care," said Grizz.

Ursine pulled his ears out to the side, then twisted them.

"Ouch! That hurt!" he yelped.

"Well, *obviously*. That was the whole point, meatbag," Grizz replied. "Now hurry up. Do the thing."

Ursine blinked. "The thing?"

"With the machine. Finish the machine. Switch it on."

"Oh. Oh, yes. Sorry, still half asleep," Ursine mumbled.

He slapped himself in the face five times, one after the other.

"Awake now?" asked Grizz.

Ursine nodded quickly. "Yes! Wide-awake. You can stop now," he squeaked. "Please."

Ursine poked himself in the eye.

"The machine," Grizz instructed from inside Ursine's head. "Finish it."

"Of course. Give me a moment," said Ursine. He switched on the desk light and set to work.

It didn't take long to connect the central console with the fiber-optic transmission unit. It was really just a case of plugging a stick-out bit into a stick-in bit and tightening a couple of screws.

Once he'd finished, Ursine stood back to admire his handiwork. "There."

"Is that it?" demanded Grizz.

Ursine nodded. "I installed the backup of your personality on to the emitter, as requested. It wasn't easy, because the emitter is actually much smaller than—"

"Don't care," Grizz told him. "Just tell me . . . will it work?"

"Uh, well . . . ," began Ursine. He licked a finger and held it up for a moment, then nodded. "We can access the Underground wireless network from here. That will relay the signal via the airwaves and then the phone lines to—"

THWACK!

"Yes." Ursine sighed. "Yes, it will work. It will bring the bears to life." He squirmed uncomfortably. "And . . . it will make them just like you."

"Great! Then fire it up," said Grizz. "Those meatbags are going to pay."

Ursine nodded uncertainly. "Uh, which particular 'meatbags' are you referring to?"

Ursine felt the chip in his head tremble with excitement. Grizz's voice rang out like a giggle of glee.

"*All* of them."

Lisa Marie looked around the classroom and gave a nod of approval. It wasn't perfect—it would never be perfect—but it was much tidier than it had been half an hour ago.

The toys were all put away in the cupboard, the drawing paper was neatly stacked up, workbooks had been returned to each child's drawer, and the dirty dishes had all been washed, dried and put away.

There was still some sand on the floor, but only because they weren't allowed to use the vacuum cleaner.

It was, Lisa Marie, thought, a job well done. It hadn't been as much fun as extra math, of course, but once she'd gotten into it, she had found herself quite enjoying it.

The same couldn't be said for Vernon. He was red-faced, sweaty, and slightly stooped from lifting all the plastic tubs filled with Lego. Drake was fine, having done absolutely nothing useful the whole time.

He'd offered to clean the mixing bowls the younger children had used to make cakes, but that was just an excuse to scrape all the sweet-tasting batter that clung to the bowls' sides.

Lisa Marie had taken great pleasure in pointing out that as it had been mixed by four- and five-year-olds, it almost certainly contained boogers.

Drake had turned a sort of boogery-green himself after that, and had spent the rest of detention sitting in the corner reading picture books, trying not to be sick.

The door opened and Drake jumped up from the beanbag he'd been lounging on for the past ten minutes. He brushed his hands together as if wiping away dust and grime.

"There. Job done," he announced as Miss

Watson poked her head into the room. "Oh, hi, miss," he said innocently. "Didn't see you there."

"Well!" said Miss Watson, stepping inside. "I'm impressed. This place is as good as new. You've all worked very hard."

"Not *all* of us," Lisa Marie muttered.

"Yeah," agreed Drake. "Vern here didn't really pull his weight."

"Wha—?" wheezed Vernon, too exhausted to even finish the word properly.

"I'm sure everyone did their fair share," Miss Watson said. "And more importantly, I'm sure you've all learned your lesson. I'll have no more tomfoolery, horseplay or misbehavior in my class. Is that clear?"

"Yes, miss," said Lisa Marie. She liked the word *tomfoolery,* and made a mental note to say it out loud a few times later when she was back home.

"Boys?"

"Oh yeah, totally," said Drake. "I'm a reformed man. Straight and narrow for me from here on in."

Miss Watson's sigh told him she didn't believe this for a second. The teacher peered over at Vernon next, who could only nod and give a thumbs-up in reply.

"Very good," she said, holding the door wide open. "Then you may—"

THUMP.

A sound came from inside the toy cupboard. It was soft but unmissable in the silence of the empty school.

Miss Watson flicked her gaze at the children. "What was that?" she asked.

"I don't know, miss," Lisa Marie admitted. "Probably just something falling over."

"Hmm. Yes," the teacher agreed. "Well, good-bye, everyone. I trust I won't be seeing any of you in detention for a long—"

THUMP.

The sound came again. Louder this time. More insistent.

THUMP.

THUMP.

THUMP.

Lisa Marie felt the hairs on her arm prick up and a shiver run down her spine.

No. She was being silly. It was nothing. Just some poor stacking by Vernon that meant everything inside the cupboard was now falling over.

Repeatedly falling over.

And thumping against the door.

She shot Vernon a sideways glance and was alarmed to find him looking as worried as she was.

"Is there someone in there?" demanded Miss Watson.

"Yeah, miss, it's Vernon," said Drake. He jabbed a thumb in Vernon's direction and grinned. "This one's just a hologram."

"Hilarious, Drake," said Miss Watson as she strode across to the toy cupboard. "You should have your own comedy show on TV."

Drake puffed up with pride. "You think so, miss?"

"Yes. Then I could switch you off," Miss Watson replied. She took hold of the door handle, and Lisa Marie's tummy twisted in panic.

"Miss, wait! I'm not sure you should do that!"

"Why? Who have you hidden in here?" Miss

Watson demanded. "No, in fact, don't tell me. I'll find out for myself."

She pulled open the door. Lisa Marie held her breath. . . .

Nothing happened.

A box of toy cars had toppled over on the middle shelf. As they all watched, a car rolled out of the plastic tub and hit the floor at Miss Watson's feet. Had the door been closed, the car would have thumped into it instead.

Lisa Marie breathed out with relief.

"What slapdash stacking," Miss Watson complained. She bent to retrieve the fallen car, and had just straightened up when a dozen teddy bears jumped down from the top shelf, whooping and cheering as they swarmed around her.

Miss Watson squealed in fright as the bears clung to her, thumping her with their little paws and laughing their little heads off.

Drake snorted in amusement. The frown on the top half of his face said he wasn't really sure what was going on, but the grin on the bottom half said he was loving it all the same.

"Leave her alone!" yelled Lisa Marie. She hurried to help Miss Watson, then leaped back when one of the bears pulled down a stack of boxes. The other bears scattered too, just as dozens of toy cars, lumps of clay and books came crashing down on Miss Watson, burying the teacher.

Vernon's mouth flapped open and closed in terror. He tried to speak, but all that came out was a sort of *buh-buh* noise that didn't help anyone.

Miss Watson had the good sense not to move. She lay still under the mound of toys, completely frozen in terror.

The bears, having had their fun with the teacher, turned their attention to the children. They snarled, showing pointy teeth, and held up their paws to reveal tiny sharp claws.

Most of the bears had been in the kindergarten toy cupboard for years. They'd been old and worn when Vernon and Drake had been in the class, and some of them were held together with clumsy stitches and colourful patches that were older than Lisa Marie.

"One down, three to go," spat one particularly threadbare specimen.

"Cool, it talks! Are these more of them robot bears?" Drake wondered. "Like the ones we blew up? Can we blow these up too?"

"I'd like to see you try," growled a tubby little ted with faded orange fur. His voice was low and gruff, and he sounded angry.

He wore a rain boot on his left foot and a roller skate on his right. He had a pink tutu, a cowboy-style jacket and a miniature red baseball cap saying *Grin and Bear It!* on his head.

There was something on his back too, Lisa Marie noticed. But it wasn't until he raised himself into the air and came bobbing toward her that she realized he was wearing a set of fairy wings.

"We have to get out of here," whispered Lisa Marie as she and Vernon backed away. Drake watched the flying teddy as it fluttered toward him. "Oh, that is so cool!" he said. "I am *definitely* going to blow this one up."

The flying bear jammed a paw up Drake's nose. For a moment, it looked like Drake was about to sneeze, but then the bear flipped Drake over his shoulder and sent him crashing into a stack of chairs.

The other teddies fanned out across the floor, giggling menacingly. In the middle of the pack, the cheerleader teddy did a high kick and waved her pom-poms above her head.

"Teddies, teddies, here's our plan," she sang. Then she pointed to Lisa Marie, Vernon and the upside-down Drake. Her mouth curved up into an angry snarl. "Gobble them up, as fast as you can!"

6

"They're back!" wailed Vernon, finally remembering how to speak. "How do they always come back?"

He and Lisa Marie stumbled out of the kindergarten classroom, each holding one of Drake's legs. They skidded into the corridor and ducked just as a book of fairy tales flew over their heads. This was followed by a few Lego bricks, a plastic kettle and three toy trucks.

From inside the classroom came the sound of chairs being broken, toys being thrown and a general clattering chaos. A pot of paint bounced into the corridor, splattering the walls with purple blobs. A bag of flour came next. It exploded against the ceiling, releasing a dusty white cloud.

Drake watched all this from flat on his back, so everything looked upside down. He didn't know what was going on exactly, but he was sure he didn't like it.

"What are you two idiots doing?" he demanded, kicking both legs. "Let me go!"

"Shut up and keep running!" Lisa Marie barked.

"What do you mean 'keep running'? I'm not running! You're pulling me," Drake pointed out.

Lisa Marie looked down at the foot tucked under her arm, as if only just seeing it for the first time. "Oh. Right. Yes," she said, dropping the foot. Vernon followed suit.

"About time," Drake snapped. He got to his feet and dusted himself off. "Now, what's the story with these robot bears? Why did that one chuck me over its . . . ? Hey, wait!" he cried as Lisa Marie and Vernon took off again. He was about to shout something suitably horrible at them, when he heard some squeaking, some boinging and the soft *pitter-patter* of footsteps from behind.

Drake turned and saw dozens of bears hurtling along the corridor toward him. Some of them ran. A few rode tricycles. Two hopped on a pogo stick. The bear with the fairy wings fluttered along in front, bobbing unsteadily. Reaching into its boot, the bear produced a pink wand with a glittery star on the top. With a mischievous grin, the bear flicked its wrist and a ball of white light streaked from the end of the wand.

Drake ducked, then watched as the light hit the school trophy cabinet farther along the corridor. The cabinet instantly began to melt, like chocolate on a warm day, dripping and oozing until it was a puddle on the floor.

With a gulp, Drake turned back to the fast-approaching bears. "Uh-oh," he muttered. Lisa Marie and Vernon were just rounding a corner up ahead when Drake came sprinting past them, his eyes wide with fear. "Look out! Coming through! Move! Move!" he cried.

He quickly drew ahead, then slowed just

enough for Lisa Marie and Vernon to catch up. "Okay, first, what's going on with these robots?" Drake demanded. "And second, where are we going?"

"Not robots. Evil teddies," Lisa Marie puffed. It didn't exactly answer Drake's first question, but it was the best she could offer right now. As for where they were going . . . ? "Anywhere but here," she suggested.

"Fire exit!" Vernon yelped, pointing to a door ahead.

Drake shot off again, powering toward the fire exit. Just before he could reach for the push-down bar, another ball of light streaked past him and the door became a wall of solid brick.

Drake ran straight into it.

"Ow!" he cried.

A moment later, Vernon and Lisa Marie ran into him.

"Ow!"

"This way!" Lisa Marie cried, grabbing the boys and stumbling into a side corridor as the tricycle bears came pedaling furiously behind them.

"Where are we going?" asked Vernon. "The way out is back there!"

"Yes, through the bears," Lisa Marie pointed out. "Be my guest if you want to try it. I'm going to find somewhere to hide."

"Hide?" Drake sneered. For a moment, Lisa Marie thought he was going to act all tough and say something about how he wasn't going to hide from any stupid teddy bears, but then he nodded. "Okay, I'm in. Hide where?"

A smell hit Lisa Marie as they skidded around another corridor. A smell that turned her stomach and made her want to run screaming in the opposite direction.

It was the smell of school lunches.

"This way," she urged, heading for the double doors that led into the cafeteria. Drake raced ahead again, threw the doors open and hurried inside. The doors swung back and clattered into Lisa Marie and Vernon, almost knocking them off their feet.

"Thanks a lot," Lisa Marie hissed, hurrying inside and carefully swinging the doors back into position.

She strained her ears for any sign of the bears. Hopefully she and the boys had made it into the cafeteria without being spotted. If they stayed quiet, the teddies should run right past. Then they could sneak back to the kindergarten classroom, check on Miss Watson and make their escape.

"Nobody make a sound," Lisa Marie whispered, ducking so she wasn't visible through the small glass panels in the doors. From outside came the squeaking of tricycle pedals and the rubbery *boing* of a pogo stick getting closer and closer.

"Um," said Drake.

"Shh," Lisa Marie urged. "Quiet."

"No, but . . ."

Lisa Marie and Vernon both turned to him.

"Will you *please* shut—" Lisa Marie began.

Then she saw what Drake was trying to tell

them. A teddy bear in a chef's outfit was standing on the serving counter, a shocked expression on its adorable face.

Lisa Marie had completely forgotten about Cafeteria Dan. He usually stood behind the small tabletop blackboard that the lunch ladies wrote the day's menu on, and was sort of the cafeteria mascot. There were laminated notices on the walls with phrases like *Cafeteria Dan says: Eat your greens!* and a little picture of Dan's friendly face accompanying each one.

Lisa Marie held out a hand slowly, as if trying to tame a lion. She pleaded to Cafeteria Dan with her eyes as the corridor beyond the door was filled with the squeaking, boinging and angry shouts of the teddy-bear pack.

Cafeteria Dan looked from the children to the door, then back again, saying nothing. Lisa Marie smiled at him. He'd always seemed like such a nice bear. Like he only had the children's best interests at heart. She hoped that was still true.

"Well, hey there, guys!" chirped Dan in a bright, cheerful voice.

From behind his back, he produced a metal ladle. He swished it around like a club, then pointed it at them and snarled:

"Say hello to my little friend!"

Cafeteria Dan kicked over the blackboard, sending it clattering to the floor. The sound echoed around the empty cafeteria, and the chatter of the bears out in the corridor rose excitedly as they doubled back.

"Aw, no!" Vernon groaned. "They're coming! What do we do? What do we do?"

Lisa Marie grabbed her stepbrother by his sweater. "First of all, do *not* faint," she warned. "Secondly, duck."

Vernon frowned? "Huh?" he said.

A second later, a flying frying pan thrown by Cafeteria Dan conked him on the back of the head.

"Ow!"

"Too late." Lisa Marie winced. She jabbed a finger urgently toward the double doors. "You two, barricade the entrance. And whatever you do, don't let them get in. I'll take care of Cafeteria Dan."

Vernon and Drake grabbed chairs from a stack and hurriedly wedged them under the handles of both doors just as the teddies threw themselves against the other side. The chairs shook. Vernon and Drake exchanged glances.

"More chairs," Vernon said.

Drake nodded. He looked a bit bewildered by what was going on, but he wasn't arguing. For now, at least.

While the boys hurried to add to the barricade, Lisa Marie and Cafeteria Dan circled each other in the middle of the hall. Dan swished his ladle around, snarling up at the much larger Lisa Marie. She had picked up the frying pan that Dan had thrown at Vernon, and gripped it like a tennis racket. It was quite a small pan, but then Cafeteria Dan was quite a small bear, so she hoped it would do the job.

"Why are you doing this?" Lisa Marie asked. "What's going on? How are you alive?"

"Oh, wouldn't *you* like to know?" sneered Dan.

"Well . . . yes," said Lisa Marie. "That's why I asked."

Cafeteria Dan lunged with the ladle and swung it at Lisa Marie's knee. There was a loud, hollow *clank* as she blocked it with the frying pan.

Spinning around, Dan swung the ladle at the other knee. Lisa Marie stepped back, avoiding it.

"You're well trained," Dan observed.

"Not really," said Lisa Marie, shrugging. "I just have a lot of experience fighting teddy bears."

Vernon yelped in fright as the doors shook. Lisa Marie glanced over, giving Cafeteria Dan just the opportunity he needed. He lunged, swinging and snarling. The ladle connected hard with Lisa Marie's ankle, making her cry out in pain.

"Ha!" snorted Dan. "Not so good at fighting teddy bears now, are y—?"

THWANG!

The frying pan slammed into him, lifting him off his paws and sending him hurtling through the air. The next moment, he plummeted out of sight behind the serving counter.

"Oh, I don't know. I think I've still got it," said Lisa Marie, giving the frying pan a little victory twirl.

She limped over to join Vernon and Drake, who were shoving against the barricade with all their strength, desperately trying to stop the bears from getting through.

"It's no use," Vernon groaned, his face turning

a funny red color with the effort. "They're too strong!"

"They're teddy bears," Lisa Marie pointed out. "Not elephants."

Drake glowered at her. "Well, *you* try to hold it then!" he said, jumping clear.

Vernon gave a cry of fright and braced himself harder against the stack of chairs.

"You idiot!" Lisa Marie snapped, leaping to take Drake's place.

She was about to start pushing when she realized there was no need. The door was no longer moving. The bears had stopped trying to get through.

"Vernon," she said.

"*Nnng!*" Vernon strained, his face going from red to purple. "*Unnng!*"

"Vernon! You can stop!" Lisa Marie told him. "They're not coming anymore."

Vernon relaxed, just a little, worried this was all a trick to make them drop their guard. He risked a peek through the little window. Other than an abandoned tricycle and a pogo stick, the corridor outside was empty.

The teddies had gone.

"Where are they?" he whispered.

"I don't know," Lisa Marie admitted.

Drake punched a fist into the opposite palm. "All right, is someone going to tell me what's going on?" he demanded. "Or do I have to start cracking skulls?"

"Shut up," Lisa Marie hissed.

Drake's face darkened. "What did you just say?"

"Shh!" Lisa Marie urged, waving the frying pan menacingly. "Listen."

Vernon and Drake both listened.

"I don't hear anything," said Drake.

And then he did. It was barely audible over the sound of Vernon's panicky breathing.

CREAK.

One by one, all three children looked up. A

few of the ceiling tiles were trembling, although not as badly as Vernon was.

"Run," Lisa Marie whispered.

Drake was still staring at the ceiling. The look on his face said he hadn't figured out what was going on, and probably wasn't likely to any time soon.

"Run!" Lisa Marie cried, shoving him toward the barricaded doors. As she did, the ceiling tiles collapsed, and a gang of teddies came tumbling into the cafeteria.

Vernon and Drake tore frantically at the barricade, tossing aside the chairs as they tried to unblock the exit.

A few yards away, Lisa Marie swung her frying pan. *THWAM!* A teddy bear flew across the cafeteria. He thumped against one of the windows, groaned loudly, then fell face-first to the floor.

The other bears closed in on Lisa Marie. The cheerleader bear was about to launch into another chant, but a solid kick to her pudgy belly fired her into the far corner of the room before she could get out her first *rah-rah-rah*.

"Not cheering about that, are you?" Lisa

Marie muttered. "Vernon, Drake, hurry up and get the doors open!"

"We're working on it!" Vernon yelped.

A tatty old teddy that looked older than Lisa Marie grabbed her leg. It opened its mouth wide and tried to bite her ankle, but the bear was so ancient it didn't have any teeth.

"Get off, you geriatric fuzzball!" Lisa Marie protested, swinging her leg back and forth until the bear lost its grip and tumbled off to join the cheerleader.

Another bear leaped on her from above. She couldn't see this one, but from the way it giggled as it pulled her hair, she knew it was younger and stronger than the last one, and almost certainly had a full set of teeth.

Lisa Marie tried to thwack it with the frying pan, but the bear scampered across her back, dodging the swipe. "Missed me!" it hissed, then yelped as it was wrenched away by one of its legs.

"Maybe. But I didn't," Vernon told the bear. He swung it around his head several times before hurling it across the cafeteria and into the kitchen area.

"Thanks," said Lisa Marie.

Vernon nodded. "No problem."

"Are you going to help me or what?" Drake demanded, struggling to move the last couple of chairs. They were wedged tightly under the handles of the doors, and it took both him and Vernon to shift them while Lisa Marie fought back the bears with the frying pan.

"Okay, got it," Vernon said, pulling open one of the doors.

Drake hurried through first. "Out of my way!"

"Lisa Marie, hurry!" Vernon called, beckoning his stepsister to follow him.

With a final *clang* that flattened a teddy to the floor, Lisa Marie turned and followed Drake out of the cafeteria, with Vernon hot on her heels.

As Lisa Marie and Vernon raced along the corridor, a ball of magical light shot past them. It whistled through the gap between them, missing them by inches.

They watched as the magical blast continued along the corridor.

"Drake, look—" Lisa Marie began, but her warning came too late.

The blast of magic struck Drake in the middle of his back. For a moment, his whole body seemed to light up, showing his skeleton.

There was a *BANG*.

There was a puff of smoke.

And then, through the smoke, there came another sound. A sound Lisa Marie and Vernon had both heard many times before.

"Quack."

As they raced through the smoky corridor, the children saw a duck standing at the far end. It was staring down at its webbed feet in confusion.

"He's turned into a duck," said Vernon, stating the obvious.

"Drake," said Lisa Marie, glancing nervously back at the chasing pack of bears. The bear with the fairy wand was bobbing along in front, lining up for another shot.

"Yes. Drake. Who else would, I mean?" Vernon asked.

"I mean, he's a drake. A male duck," Lisa Marie said. "You can tell from the color of—"

"Is this really the best time for a nature lesson?!" Vernon cried.

"It's always a good time for a nature lesson," Lisa Marie said. "But I take your point. Grab him!"

Vernon bent down and snatched Drake up, narrowly avoiding the second magical bolt. It exploded on the wall ahead of them, turning it into a cloud of sparkly confetti.

"There's our way out!" Lisa Marie cried.

"Go, go, go!" Vernon yelped.

"Quack," said Drake, who couldn't really add a lot else at this point.

"Get back here, meatbags!" barked one of the bears.

Lisa Marie turned and stared, her eyes widening with horror. "What did that teddy just say?" she whispered.

"No time for that now," panted Vernon. He caught his stepsister by the arm and pulled her outside onto the playground.

They both screamed, and Drake made a panicky honk sound as a white van with the word PIZZA on the side almost knocked them down. It screeched to a stop just inches in front of them. A side door slid open and a man in a dark suit and sunglasses beckoned them inside.

"Want a lift?" asked Agent Strong.

"Wouldn't say no," gasped Lisa Marie. She and Vernon jumped into the van and the door slid closed.

"Go!" barked Agent Strong as the teddies came tumbling through the school gates. The van's tires spun, then it sped off in a cloud of burning rubber, throwing Lisa Marie and Vernon into the same seats they'd been in earlier.

"Nice duck," the agent said, sitting on the desk and bracing himself against the side of the van.

Vernon looked down at the bird in his arms. "Yeah, it's—"

"Don't care," said Agent Strong, holding a hand up to silence him. "We have a problem."

"We noticed," said Lisa Marie.

"We noticed that you noticed," said Agent Strong. "We've been monitoring you."

"Espionage!" said Lisa Marie. Mostly because she liked the word. She clarified it before Vernon could even ask. "You've been spying on us!"

"Of course we have," said Agent Strong. "We're the government. We spy on everyone. And the situation is worse than you think. It isn't confined to your school. Teddy bears are coming to life all over the country. It's chaos. We need your help."

"Our *help*?" Vernon gasped. "You're the government. You've got the police and the army! We're just a couple of kids."

"*Quack.*"

"Okay, a couple of kids and a duck," Vernon said.

"You're also the only people who have

experience dealing with these bears," Agent Strong pointed out.

Lisa Marie shook her head. "Vernon's right. We can't stop them."

"You can't?" asked Agent Strong.

"We can't?" asked Vernon, who had never known Lisa Marie to give up so quickly before.

"Quack?" asked Drake, mainly because he didn't want to be left out.

Lisa Marie folded her arms and shot Agent Strong her sternest look. "No. There's nothing we can do," she said. The beginnings of a grin crept across her face. "At least, not without a little help from the King!"

Ursine Kodiak shuffled along a London street, his eyes growing wider with wonder at all the people running around in panic.

Police sirens screamed in the distance. Helicopters hovered overhead. A black cab came skidding past him, tires screeching. Ursine watched as it smashed into a lamppost and smoke billowed from under the hood.

A moment later, the cab driver jumped out, a teddy bear holding on to his ears and thumping him repeatedly over the head with its tiny paws.

A little farther along the street, the window of a toy shop exploded outward and dozens of teddy bears came spilling on to the pavement. They gnashed their teeth and snarled at the terrified pedestrians, waving their claws as they chased them away, racing along on their stumpy little legs.

None of them paid Ursine the slightest bit of

attention as he strolled past, supporting himself on a cane. When he'd built his machine, he'd made sure to program himself in as a friend of the teddies so they wouldn't attack him.

"Remarkable," Ursine whispered. "I did it. I actually did it."

"*I* did it," snarled Grizz inside Ursine's head.

"But bringing teddies to life was originally my idea," Ursine protested.

"If it wasn't for me, you'd have failed miserably," Grizz replied. "And now look—every single teddy bear in the country is alive and kicking."

"With your personality," Ursine added, biting anxiously on his bottom lip.

THWACK!

"Not *all* my personality, just parts of it," Grizz snapped. "Ain't no one else quite like me, and don't you forget that."

"Yes . . . sorry . . . yes," Ursine muttered, rubbing his aching cheek.

Ursine stepped aside to let a woman run past. She was being chased by a teddy bear in a frog outfit. It hopped after her, its long tongue snapping at her heels.

"I say," Ursine remarked.

He looked around at some of the other bears currently causing chaos. A few bears dressed like baseball players had set up a game right in the middle of the street. The batsman was deliberately whacking balls at the windows of surrounding buildings, and shouting, "Owzat?" whenever they smashed one. A cowboy bear was busily rounding up tourists with a lasso, while a teddy dressed like a maid was chasing children with a feather duster and laughing like a maniac.

"They're taking on some element of their apparel," Ursine said. "Just like with the Halloween bears."

He slapped himself in the face.

"English," snarled Grizz.

"Sorry. I mean, they're behaving like the clothes they're wearing," said Ursine. "Whatever the outfit, they take on some of its wearer's characteristics. How fascinating."

"Fascinating, shmascinating," Grizz grunted. "Who cares? They're running riot, and that's all that matters."

Ursine's hand came up suddenly. At first, he thought Grizz was going to make him slap himself again, but then two of the fingers jammed into his mouth and he let out a whistle. The baseball-playing bears stopped their game and hurried over to gather in front of Ursine. They stared up at him expectantly.

"Er, hello," Ursine said, but then he felt a strange tingling in his brain and an odd sort of warmth pass through his eyes.

The baseball bears stiffened for a moment, then nodded their understanding. "Yes, master. Of course, master," they chirped as they hurried past Ursine and raced back in the direction he'd come from.

"They somehow sense you in my head. They realize that I'm their master," Ursine noted. "How very interesting."

He twisted his nose, then pulled both ears.

"They know *I'm* their master," said Grizz. "Just like you better start remembering that I'm yours."

"S-sorry," Ursine stammered.

A police helicopter roared overhead, spinning out of control as hundreds of bears hung on below it. Somewhere in the distance, something exploded, and one of the many sirens that had been wailing nearby suddenly changed direction to investigate.

Ursine's feet plodded along the street. "Where are we going?" he asked. "You said you'd let me go once I'd built the machine. You said you just wanted to cause chaos."

"Chaos is fun, but I've decided to aim my sights higher," said Grizz. "Why settle for messing up the world when I can lock up all the meatbags and lead the teddies in a worldwide takeover? But for that I need you to build something else for me. Something *big*."

Ursine whimpered, then gestured around the street. The people had all been chased away now, and the road was filled with abandoned cars, toppled motorcycles and hundreds of celebrating teddy bears.

"How am I supposed to build anything here?" he asked.

His feet walked faster, until he was jerking along like a puppet.

"Not here," Grizz said. They reached the end of the street and turned sharply left. "There!"

Ursine let out a gasp of surprise. "You can't be serious," he whispered.

"I'm deadly serious," said Grizz. "Now, say hello to our new home."

Ursine swallowed. There, directly ahead of them, was Buckingham Palace. Police cars and army trucks formed a barricade in front of the entrance, the flashing blue lights from the cars licking across the tall metal gates. Officers and soldiers stood guard, their eyes darting anxiously at the surrounding streets.

Ursine ducked back into cover, out of sight.

"This isn't our home. It's the Queen's," he whispered.

Inside his head, Grizz gave a snigger. "Not anymore."

Lisa Marie paced back and forth in a small room, her own reflection pacing alongside her in a mirror that ran from one end of a wall to the other.

Vernon sat at a table, anxiously chewing his nails and trying hard not to faint.

Drake ruffled his feathers, quacked sadly, then did a sneaky poo in the corner.

They had been driven in the van for over an hour. Agent Strong had assured them that their parents were being kept safe at what he called "a government facility," but after more questioning he'd admitted they were really at the local community center. An emergency shelter had been set up there, and half the town was gathered in it for protection.

Vernon looked up at his stepsister as she paced across the room.

"Can you stop that?" he asked. "You're making me nervous."

"You were already nervous," Lisa Marie pointed out. She reached one wall, turned and started back the way she'd come. "This isn't making you any worse."

Vernon wanted to argue, but he knew she was right. Lisa Marie could sit, walk, run—even do a handstand—and he'd still be exactly as worried as he was now.

"They can't keep us locked up here," he said, studying the wall mirror. He reckoned it was one of those two-way mirrors that let people look through from the other side, like they had on TV detective shows. He made a face at it, just in case anyone was watching. "Can they?"

"They're the government," said Lisa Marie. "I think they can pretty much do whatever they want."

This was not what Vernon wanted to hear.

Jumping up, he banged both fists against the mirror. "You can't keep us here!" he yelled. "Let us go! We have rights, you know? We've been here for hours!"

"Minutes," Lisa Marie corrected him.

"Really?" asked Vernon. He hesitated. "It seems longer. How do you know?"

"There's a clock up there," Lisa Marie said, pointing. "It's been about eight minutes."

Vernon regarded the clock. "Oh," he said. Then he shrugged and went back to hammering his fists on the glass. "Let us out. We demand our phone call!"

"Quack," agreed Drake.

The door on the other side of the room opened. Agent Strong entered but stopped when he saw Vernon hammering on the glass.

"What are you doing?" he asked, frowning over the top of his sunglasses. "You know that's just a normal mirror, right?"

Vernon and his reflection both frowned. "Is it? Oh. I thought you were spying on us."

"We were. With that camera," said Agent Strong, pointing to a camera fixed to the wall in one corner of the room. A red light blinked steadily on top of it. "Take a seat," he said, gesturing to the chairs.

"No!" yelled Lisa Marie. "You said you were going to get Bearvis. You promised. So where—?"

"Outta the way, you big hunka nothin'," came a voice from the corridor.

Lisa Marie sprang forward so fast and so suddenly that Agent Strong instinctively leaped out of the doorway, rolled across the floor and sprang to his feet in a karate stance.

"That was actually pretty cool," Vernon admitted.

"Quack," agreed Drake.

Lisa Marie reached the doorway just as a bear in a white jumpsuit covered in sequins reached it from the other side. She snatched Bearvis up in a hug and spun with him on the spot, crying hot, happy tears of relief.

"Bearvis! You're alive!" she cheered.

"Sure am, little darlin'," the teddy drawled. "But I just had lunch, and I ain't sure my stomach can handle much more of this spinning."

Lisa Marie stopped twirling him around and inspected him closely. "I was afraid they might have dissected you," she said.

"Nuh-uh," said Bearvis. "The King's all in one piece, honey." He glanced up at his hair, which still had a hole burned through it from an encounter with an alien bear's ray gun. "Well, mostly. Fact is, they treated me just fine. Heck, the kitchen even added my favorite meal to the menu—fried peanut-butter-and-banana sandwich."

"Ew," said Vernon.

"Don't knock it till you've tried it, son," Bearvis said. He winked at Vernon. "Good to see you too."

The next few minutes were swallowed up by Lisa Marie, Vernon and Bearvis chatting about the past few days, and by Agent Strong sighing impatiently and checking his watch. Drake was beginning to feel that no one was taking the whole duck situation seriously enough, and quacked loudly to get everyone's attention.

"Hey, nice duck," said Bearvis, suddenly noticing him.

"It's Drake," Lisa Marie explained.

"Oh," said Bearvis. "That horrible kid?"

"*Quack!*" Drake protested.

"Yeah, him," Vernon confirmed.

Bearvis considered this for a moment, then went on with his previous conversation.

He explained that the Duds—the bears Ursine Kodiak had rejected when making his bear army but who had ended up helping to stop his villainous plan—were all safe, and now working with emergency services to coordinate rescue teams across the country.

"This is seriously happening all over the country?" Lisa Marie fretted.

"See for yourself," said Agent Strong. He gestured to the mirror and an image the size of a large TV screen appeared in the center.

"Ha! I *knew* it wasn't a normal mirror," Vernon said. He frowned. "I mean, normal mirrors don't do that, do they?"

Lisa Marie shook her head and shushed him. The screen showed video taken from a security camera. People were running in fear as hundreds of teddy bears chased after them waving tiny weapons.

"Where is this?" Lisa Marie asked.

"Birmingham," replied Agent Strong.

The image changed. A truck zigzagged along a street, smashing through parked cars. Teddies clung to the roof and doors. Through the windshield, Lisa Marie could see the driver wrestling with a large blue bear wearing a flowery dress.

"Newcastle," Agent Strong told them.

The picture changed five or six times, with each image showing more terror, more destruction and a lot more bears.

"Bristol. Aberdeen. Cardiff."

"They're everywhere," Lisa Marie whispered. "How can they be everywhere? And what do they want?"

"As far as we can tell so far, they just want to cause chaos," replied Strong. "And as much damage as possible."

"Wait! Wait! Go back one," urged Vernon.

Agent Strong didn't move, but the screen flicked back to the previous image.

"Where is this?" Vernon asked, stepping closer to the mirror. The screen showed a street filled with teddies. They were jumping on crashed cars, swinging from lampposts and generally causing havoc.

"London," said Agent Strong. "Where we are now. Why?"

Lisa Marie gasped. "London? How can we be in London? We weren't driving long enough."

Agent Strong shrugged. "It's a fast van," he said a little enigmatically. "We're at a secure government facility."

"What kind of secure government facility?" asked Lisa Marie.

"That's classified," said Strong. He turned to Vernon before Lisa Marie could interrupt him again. "What's special about this picture?"

Vernon stepped closer still and tapped a spot on the image near the bottom right-hand corner. A head was just visible in the shot. A human head.

A *very familiar* human head.

"Hey, I know that guy," said Bearvis.

"Ursine Kodiak!" yelped Lisa Marie. "That's Ursine Kodiak. That's the man who invented the technology to bring bears to life."

"Are you sure?" asked Agent Strong.

"Quack," said Drake, because he hadn't said anything in a while and wanted to remind everyone that he was still a duck.

"I'm sure. He's pretty recognizable," Lisa Marie confirmed. "Where was this taken?"

"Like I said, London," said Agent Strong.

"Where *specifically*?" Lisa Marie demanded. "Maybe we can figure out where he's going."

The screen changed to show a map of London. They all watched in silence as it zoomed in on a spot near the center of the city. Vernon tilted his head so he could read the name of the street.

"Buckingham Palace Road," he said. He looked at the others. "Is there anything interesting around there?"

They all waited for the penny to drop.

"Oh! Buckingham Palace," said Vernon. "Gotcha. He wouldn't be going there, though, would he?"

"Ursine said he wanted to take over the world. Breaking into the palace seems like a good place to start!" said Lisa Marie.

Agent Strong shook his head. "Impossible. It's too heavily guarded."

"Can we see it?" asked Lisa Marie. "Are there cameras?"

Strong glanced at the ceiling. "Patch us into a live feed of the palace," he instructed.

For a moment, nothing happened. When the screen eventually changed, a hush fell over the room.

Several seconds passed as everyone stared at the screen.

"Quack," said Drake finally.

"Aw, man, you can say that again," Bearvis mumbled.

On-screen, police cars and army trucks had

been tipped over onto their sides. Beyond them, the tall iron gates of the palace lay twisted and buckled on the ground.

"I don't think he's going to break into the palace," Vernon whispered. "I think he already has!"

Ursine Kodiak leaned on his cane, waiting for the teddies to open the grand, imposing double doors of the palace throne room. The bears in a nearby gift shop that sold Buckingham Palace memorabilia had come to life, and they were dressed as royal footmen in red jackets, white wigs and socks pulled all the way up to their knees.

Another teddy blew a fanfare on a plastic trumpet. At least, it tried to, but the noise that came out sounded more like someone breaking wind.

Getting into the palace had been easy. Grizz had made Ursine stroll right up to the police and soldiers. Then, when everyone was shouting at him, thousands of bears had come rushing from all directions and quickly overpowered the guards.

A squad of four large bears, each one almost as tall as Ursine himself, had shouldered vehicles aside to clear a path. Then dozens of smaller bears had swept Ursine up and carried him into the palace like a surfer on a wave.

Ursine had nothing against the Queen. She had always seemed quite nice. A bit too obsessed with waving for his liking, but he bore her no grudge. He was relieved to discover she wasn't at home when the bears stormed the palace.

The entire royal family had been evacuated to safety. The head butler had explained this slowly and calmly to the invading bears, without a flicker of concern. Which was impressive, considering he was being held upside down out of an upstairs window at the time.

The doors finally swung open. The fanfare farted into silence. A smile crept across Ursine's face.

"Oh my," he said.

There, before him, was the royal throne. Two royal thrones, in fact.

Ursine looked down at the bears. "For me?"

"For *me*," hissed Grizz inside Ursine's head. He jerked Ursine forward and started complaining in a voice that only his human host could hear. "Ugh. That wallpaper will have to go. Too pink. The carpet too. Who has a pink carpet? Seriously? I mean, how old is this queen? Six? Tell them to mess this place up."

"Um, mess this place up," said Ursine.

Immediately, two of the royal foot-bears rushed to the walls and began tearing at them, carving deep claw marks across the reddish-pink surfaces.

"I mean, what next?" Grizz wondered. "Unicorn curtains?"

He hobbled Ursine all the way across the throne room. Ursine wheezed and dabbed at his forehead with a handkerchief as his legs heaved him up the three steps to the raised platform where two thrones sat—one for the Queen, the other for her husband.

Grizz regarded both thrones for a moment through Ursine's eyes, then used Ursine's foot to kick one of the thrones on to the floor.

That done, he spun Ursine around and lowered him into the one remaining throne.

"This is more like it," Grizz said. To Ursine's surprise, he found his mouth speaking the words out loud.

"Whoa, did I say that?" asked Grizz. "Hey, check it out. I can make you talk! Makes sense, I guess. I can make you do anything, so why not talk too?"

"Wh-what is this?" Ursine whimpered, but then Grizz's voice took over.

"Shut up, meatbag," the teddy said, speaking with Ursine's mouth. "I'm doing the talking now."

Ursine's hand came up on its own. A finger jabbed at one of the royal foot-bears. "You," Grizz spat in Ursine's voice. "Go get a notepad and a pencil." A wicked grin crept across Ursine's face. "We're going to make a shopping list."

"Yes, sir. Right away, sir," said the foot-bear.

Ursine raised an eyebrow. Grizz's voice came out as a low, menacing growl. "Sir?"

The bear bowed as it backed toward the door. "I mean, yes, *Your Majesty*. Right away."

"Better," said Grizz. He watched the foot-bear scurry away until he was almost at the exit, then called after him, "Wait!"

The bear in the little white wig stopped, swallowed nervously, then turned. "Y-yes, Your Majesty?"

"Put me in touch with the roughest, toughest teddies you can find," Grizz said. Ursine leaned forward in the throne, making it creak beneath his weight. "I have a job for them."

Lisa Marie stared thoughtfully at the live feed from outside Buckingham Palace.

"What could they be doing in there?" she wondered.

"All kindsa no good," guessed Bearvis, who stood on Lisa Marie's shoulder.

"Can't you use satellites to spy on them?" asked Vernon, turning from the screen to Agent Strong.

Agent Strong frowned. "No."

"Why not?" asked Vernon.

"Well . . . because the palace has a roof."

Vernon nodded. "Oh. Yeah. Good point." He clicked his tongue against the back of his teeth. "Can't you use X-ray-vision mode?"

Agent Strong's frown deepened. "No."

"Why not?"

"Because there's no such thing as X-ray-vision mode." The agent sighed. He pointed to Lisa Marie. "Can we leave the thinking to her from now on?"

"Yeah, fair enough," said Vernon, who didn't have any other ideas anyway.

On-screen, hundreds of bears were forming a defensive ring around the palace. They had pushed the toppled cars and trucks into roadblock positions so nothing could drive through. Anyone trying to access the palace would have to do so on foot, and they'd be met by a very furry line of resistance.

"If Ursine's in there, and assuming he *is* the one behind this, we need to go there and stop him," Lisa Marie said.

"Who else would be behind it?" asked Agent Strong.

"Grizz," said Lisa Marie.

"I thought we blew that guy to pieces?" said Bearvis.

Lisa Marie nodded. "We did, but . . . I don't know. I just have a feeling . . ." She gave herself a shake. "Either way, we need to get inside the palace as soon as we can."

"How are we supposed to do that?" asked Vernon.

Lisa Marie shuddered. "The sewers. We go in underground."

"What?!" spluttered Vernon, sounding outraged.

"*Quack,*" said Drake, sounding even more outraged than Vernon.

"Uh, shinnying through a sewer pipe ain't really how the King rolls," Bearvis said. He smiled apologetically at Lisa Marie. "Sorry, honey. This bear ain't taking the low road."

Agent Strong pressed a finger to his ear for a moment, listening to something. He gave a nod, suggesting that the message had been received and understood. "It doesn't matter. There's no sewer access. We've checked the schematics."

Lisa Marie tutted, although she was quietly relieved that the sewers weren't an option. She hadn't liked the idea any more than the others had.

"Fine, then we'll have to go in from above. You have helicopters, right?" she asked, staring at the screen for inspiration. Suddenly she spotted something in the bottom corner. A bear in a royal footman's outfit was waving to the camera and jumping up and down as if trying to get their attention.

He had a large piece of cardboard tucked under one arm with some writing on it. Lisa Marie watched as he took it from under his arm and

lifted it above his head. As soon as he did, the message became clear.

"'Say goodbye, meatbags,'" Vernon read.

"Meatbags," Lisa Marie whispered. She bit her bottom lip. "It's got to be Grizz. It has to be."

"Who are we supposed to say goodbye to?" asked Vernon, looking around at the others. "What's that supposed to mean?"

And then, with a *BOOM* that made the whole room shake, an outer wall of the government facility exploded and an alarm began to scream.

Agent Strong jammed a finger against his ear, trying to listen to the voice in his earpiece over the sound of the alarm.

"The facility is under attack," he said.

"We figured that out!" cried Lisa Marie.

"Quack!" added Drake, flapping around in panic.

The image on-screen changed to show a bird's-eye view of a building. Smoke was pouring out of a hole in the wall as teddy bears piled in through it.

"Where is this?" Lisa Marie demanded.

Agent Strong stared at the screen in disbelief. "Uh . . . that's classified."

"It's here, isn't it?" said Lisa Marie, grabbing

him by the lapels of his suit and shaking him."It's this building!"

"Yes! Yes, it's here," admitted Agent Strong.

"Oh no! What do we do? What do we do?" yelped Vernon, hopping from foot to foot.

Bearvis somersaulted down from Lisa Marie's shoulder and stood between the children and the door, paws raised, ready to fight. "Stay behind me," he warned. "If any of those furry mommas shows their face, they're gonna get it. The King's gonna take care of business. You wait and see."

Agent Strong cleared his throat. "Or, alternatively . . ."

Behind him, the mirror slid back to reveal a hidden room beyond. "I *knew* it!" Vernon cried.

He screamed in fright as the duck flew past him, wings flapping frantically. It tumbled through the gap where the mirror had been, gave a few urgent quacks, then began pecking at a closed door at the back of the secret room.

"Go. Go. Get out of here," Agent Strong instructed, shoving Lisa Marie through the gap and tossing Vernon through after her. "I'll stay here and hold them off."

"We'll get to the palace and stop all this," Lisa Marie said.

"What? On our own?" cried Vernon. "You can't be serious."

Agent Strong shook his head. "No. It's too dangerous. There's a safe room two doors down on the right. There's no way they can get inside. Go there and hide."

"That's a much better plan," agreed Vernon.

Bearvis scampered up to Agent Strong.

"'Scuse me. Coming through," he said. Then he flipped off the agent's shoulder and landed lightly at Lisa Marie's feet. He winked up at her, before turning back to the space where the mirror had been.

"Don't worry, son. The King'll make sure they stay outta trouble," Bearvis drawled.

"See that you do," said Agent Strong. The mirror slid back into place.

There was something about the way Bearvis was grinning that made Lisa Marie suspicious.

"You didn't," she said.

Bearvis held up a set of car keys. "I did."

"Bearvis, you're a genius!" said Lisa Marie.

"Well, thank you," drawled Bearvis, swinging the keys around on his paw. "Thank you very much."

A van roared out of an underground parking garage, smashed through the barrier and briefly took to the air as it sped off the exit ramp and into the darkening streets of London.

Up front, the four occupants—two children, one teddy bear and an increasingly irate duck—were thrown around in their seats as the van clattered onto solid ground, then skidded sideways across two lanes of the road.

"Aw, man, this is fun," said Bearvis. He was

sitting on Lisa Marie's lap in the driver's seat, his paws gripping the wheel. "Okay, honey, right foot down," he instructed.

Lisa Marie pushed down on a pedal with her right foot and the van lurched forward, throwing Vernon back in his seat and sending a Summertime Forest air freshener flying into the duck's face.

"Careful!" Vernon protested. He shot Bearvis a worried look. "Do you even know how to drive?"

"Drive? Yes," said Bearvis, leaning over and crunching through the gears. "Stop? No."

Before Vernon could react, a fat furry body thudded onto the van's windshield. Its little claws slashed at the glass, carving long, jagged trenches down it.

"Don't y'all worry. The King's gonna take care of this guy, lickety-split," Bearvis said. He hummed quietly to himself as he examined the controls. "Wipers. Wipers . . ."

He clicked a switch. The van's headlights went out, plunging the road ahead into near darkness. Everyone screamed or quacked in fright.

"Well, that ain't it," Bearvis said, switching

the lights back on. He tried twisting a plastic stalk that stuck out from one side of the wheel. The stereo blared to life, making everyone jump.

Bearvis cocked his head and listened to the song that came out of the speakers. "They call that music?" he muttered, before flicking it off again.

On the windshield, the teddy continued to

gnash and claw at the glass. Lisa Marie grabbed another of the plastic stalks and gave it a twist. A set of windshield wipers flicked up. The bear's expression changed to one of surprise as it was launched sideways off the windshield and sent tumbling into the evening gloom.

Over the thrum of the van's engine, they heard the sounds of a city being torn apart. Cars crashed. People screamed. Teddies roared. None of the buildings were lit up, and the streetlights were off too, suggesting the power had been cut.

"It's like a nightmare," Vernon whispered.

Drake nodded in agreement. *"Quack."*

"Whatever you say, son," said Bearvis, shooting Drake a sideways glance.

He faced front again, then yelped in fright when he saw a double-decker bus dead ahead. Somehow, it had been flipped all the way over so it was on its roof, completely blocking the road from one side to the other.

"Everyone, hold on!" Bearvis warned, yanking the wheel to the right and sending the van into a skid."I think we're gonna—"

CRASH.

One minute, the van was moving; the next, it wasn't. Air bags popped out all around them, protecting them from the shattering glass and the jolt of the impact.

"Is everyone okay?" coughed Lisa Marie.

"I think so," Vernon groaned.

"Quack."

"Come on, we gotta move," urged Bearvis.

"You're lucky we *can* move!" snapped Vernon. "Why didn't you look where you were going?"

Bearvis raised a paw and pointed past Vernon. The airbags had started to deflate, revealing a crowd of teddy bears approaching.

"You want to argue about this now or later, son?" Bearvis drawled.

Vernon swallowed. "Later," he whimpered. "Argue later."

"Yeah, that's what I thought," said Bearvis.

He sprang forward and hit the windshield with a flying kick, knocking the glass out of its frame and on to the van's hood.

Bearvis grabbed Lisa Marie by the hand, then

urged Vernon to follow. "Come on, we gotta get moving. Hurry up," he said. "And bring the duck."

Together, they all slid down the van's hood, then tumbled to the ground. The bus was blocking the road, but the door of a craft supplies shop stood open across the street. It was the kind of shop Lisa Marie usually loved going into, although she suspected now wasn't the best time to browse.

"We can hide in there," she whispered, scooping Bearvis up in her arms. She stuck to the shadows and crept into the shop. Behind her, Vernon hurried to keep up, with Drake the duck waddling along behind him.

"Safe at last," Lisa Marie whispered, quietly closing the door.

From somewhere at the back of the shop came the sound of claws ripping through fabric, and a low, menacing growl.

"Oh," Vernon said, gulping. "You *think* so?"

"Duck!" whispered Lisa Marie.

"*Quack?*" said Drake.

"No, I didn't mean you!" said Lisa Marie. She lowered her head. "Like that."

The children, the bear and the duck all crouched and took cover behind the shop's counter, listening to the conversation going on in the storeroom.

"Is that enough?" asked a teddy with a high, squeaky voice.

"How should I know?" grunted another, much larger-sounding bear.

"Maybe we should take all of it?" the squeaky voice suggested.

"Are you kidding?" demanded the lower voice. "I might be big, but I'm not *that* big."

"He said we had to get as much as we could carry and bring it back to the palace."

"Yeah, well, this is as much as we can carry," the lower voice insisted. "If he needs more, we'll have to come back. Now let's get out of here."

There was some rustling, followed by the faint sound of teddy bear footsteps heading toward the door. Lisa Marie and Bearvis peeked out from behind the counter and watched as two very differently sized teddies made their way across the shop.

The larger bear, who was almost as tall as Lisa Marie, had a roll of furry fabric over one shoulder. The smaller bear carried a single spool of thread, and even that seemed like a bit of a struggle for him.

"Did you shut this door?" asked the larger bear, stopping by the shop's entrance.

"How would I have done that?" asked the smaller bear. "It's huge."

Lisa Marie and Vernon held their breath as
the big bear turned and looked around the shop.

"Must've been the wind," he said, pulling the
door open. Everyone waited until the bears had
left before they dared to breathe again.

Vernon let out a sigh of relief. "What are they up to?" he asked.

"Not sure," Lisa Marie admitted. "But they're going to the palace, and it sounds like something big's happening. We need to get inside."

"You saw the barricades on TV, honey. Ain't no way we can just walk in," said Bearvis.

"I have an idea," said Lisa Marie.

She tiptoed out from behind the counter and crept toward the storeroom. Bearvis scampered after her and waved his paws threateningly in the direction of the front door, just in case the bears returned.

"What are you doing?" Vernon hissed. "It could be dangerous in there."

"The whole country has been taken over by evil bears, Vernon," Lisa Marie whispered back. "*Everywhere's* dangerous."

Drake looked up at Vernon and quacked.

"I think he just called you a chicken, son," said Bearvis.

Vernon tutted. "Better a living chicken than

a dead duck," he muttered, but then he scurried after Lisa Marie, keeping low.

"Drake, stay there and be our lookout," said Lisa Marie. "If anyone comes, sound the alarm."

Vernon scoffed. "He's a duck. How's he supposed to work the alarm?"

Lisa Marie sighed and rolled her eyes. "I meant *quack loudly,* not sound the actual ala—Forget it."

She marched into the storeroom. "This way. If the plan's going to work, there's no time to lose!"

An hour later, evening had turned to night. A full moon hung in the air, shining a faint silvery glow on the streets below.

The power was out everywhere now. Other than the moon, the only light came from the headlights of cars that had been abandoned on every street. They shone like spotlights on a large mob of bears that were filing one by one through a gap in the barricade around Buckingham Palace.

The palace itself still had lights too. They burned in every window, turning the whole building into a beacon in the darkness.

"Keep coming, keep coming," urged one of the bears on the palace side of the blockade. He was dressed in a neat suit and bowler hat, and was flanked on both sides by two Queen's Guard teddies in tall bearskin helmets. The guards stared straight ahead, saying nothing.

"Hurry up. His Majesty is waiting in the ballroom," the suited bear said, beckoning the teddies through the gap. He glanced at a bear in a sparkly white jumpsuit and nodded his approval. "Nice outfit."

"Well, thank you, son," drawled the teddy, running a paw through his shiny black hair. "Thank you very much."

Bearvis strode confidently through the gap, then hung back and waited when he reached the other side.

A taller bear came through next, fumbling a

little as it felt its way along. It could best be described as odd-looking, with fur that didn't quite seem to fit properly, eyes that were made of buttons and a smile that almost looked glued on.

"Uh, are you all right?" asked the suited bear.

"Fine," replied the bear in a girl's voice. It coughed, then dropped its voice to a growl. "I mean . . . fine. But thanks for asking."

After a moment, the bear was waved through.

If that teddy had looked bad, the one behind it was even worse. It was one of the largest teddies the suited bear had ever seen, and its fur was a patchwork of different colors and fabrics, all clumsily stitched together. Its button eyes were different colors and stitched on at different heights, its nose had been drawn on in marker, its ears were two circles of cardboard, and it didn't have a mouth.

It also, for reasons the suited bear wasn't entirely clear on, carried a duck under its arm.

"What's with the bird?" the bear asked, once he had finished looking the newcomer up and down.

Inside his bear suit, Vernon panicked. He looked down at Drake but was barely able to make him out through the tiny holes he'd made in the fabric to see through.

"Well?" demanded the bear. The guards beside him shifted their gazes in Vernon's direction.

Vernon swallowed. "He's, uh, my cousin."

He bit his lip and squeaked. His *cousin?* Why on earth had he said that?! They'd see through that right away. He was dead. Doomed. Done for.

The bear in the suit looked at the duck.

He looked at the wonky-eyed, mouthless face of the towering teddy bear.

He shrugged.

"Fair enough. In you go."

Vernon blinked. "What, seriously?" he asked, before he could stop himself. "I can go in?"

Down in Vernon's arms, the duck tutted, then sighed.

"Yes, you can go in. And be quick about it!" barked the bear. "We do *not* want to keep His Majesty waiting!"

14

"Friends. Teddies. Loyal subjects. Our time has finally come!" boomed the figure at the front of the crowd. He looked like Ursine Kodiak—same beard, same bulky body, same tiny feet—but the voice that came out was someone else's.

"Grizz," whispered Lisa Marie inside her bear suit. "That's Grizz. I knew it."

"Really?" Vernon whispered back. "Wow. Impressive costume. He looks just like that Ursine Kodiak guy."

Lisa Marie rolled her eyes, but because her head was hidden by furry fabric, Vernon didn't notice.

On entering the palace, all the bears had been ushered into a long corridor that would've looked grand and impressive had the wallpaper not been ripped and all the statues not been smashed on the expensive carpet.

Lisa Marie's group stood a few rows from the front of the gathered crowd, but as most of the bears ahead of them were fairly small, they could see Ursine, or Grizz, or whoever it was, just fine.

Bearvis whistled quietly and looked around the ornate corridor. "Aw, man, this place is fit for a king," he whispered.

Vernon nodded. "Er, yeah. That's sort of the whole point. It's Buckingham Palace."

"Thanks to my genius," continued Grizz, "the whole of Great Britain has fallen. Teddy bears have taken control of England, Scotland and Wales!"

A bear at the front put up his hand. "What about Northern Ireland? That's part of Great Britain."

Lisa Marie answered before she could stop herself. "Technically, Northern Ireland isn't part of Great Britain," she said. "It's *the United Kingdom of Great Britain and Northern Ireland,* to give it its full name."

Vernon elbowed her in the ribs. Lisa Marie realized that Ursine was staring at her, a suspicious look on his face.

Lisa Marie lowered her voice to a gruff growl. "Um, so I've heard."

Ursine's eyebrows lowered into a frown. Then he shook his head and continued.

"Anyway. As I was saying, the meatbags are trying to fight back, of course, but they're outnumbered, and we caught them off guard. We'll round up the rebels and sling them all into prison.

Maybe we'll put bows in their hair and toss them around a bit. See how they like it!"

A cheer went up at that.

"Yeah!"

"See how they like it!"

"Stupid meatbags!"

Vernon felt that he should probably join in. He waved a fist in the air and cheered, "Yay for teddies!" at the top of his voice.

An awkward silence fell. The bears nearby shot him funny looks. Even Bearvis looked a little embarrassed. Vernon blushed inside his bear suit as he felt the weight of Ursine's stare on him.

"No, not 'Yay for teddies,'" growled Grizz through Ursine's mouth. "Yay for *me*."

Vernon cleared his throat softly. "Er, yes," he whimpered. "That's what I meant. Yay for you."

"Better," Grizz said. Ursine's eyes flicked up and down, studying Vernon. "Nice duck," he said at last.

Drake opened his mouth to offer a quack in reply, but then thought better of it. At the front of the crowd, Grizz folded Ursine's hands behind him and paced back and forth between the corridor walls.

"But it's not enough. It's not nearly enough. Yes, we control this country, but it's a big world out there, and we don't control that."

Ursine's face became a bear-like snarl. "And it's not good enough."

"So, what do we do?" asked another of the bears.

Ursine's hand came up and pointed to a set of wide double doors that led off from the corridor. "We move to Phase Two," said Grizz. "And it begins through there."

The bears murmured excitedly.

"Aw, man, I got a bad feeling about this," Bearvis groaned.

Ursine's hands clapped twice. The doors creaked open beside him, pulled by four royal foot-bears. The teddies closest to the front let out little gasps of excitement as the contents of the room were revealed. Lisa Marie leaned forward, struggling to see.

Luckily, she didn't have long to wait. Ursine motioned for them to enter and a group of Queen's Guard bears appeared behind them, prodding and poking them in the back.

Lisa Marie, Vernon and Bearvis all stopped as they reached the door. They stared into the room beyond. For once Lisa Marie was lost for words.

The room was long and wide, with a high ceiling from which hung a number of impressive chandeliers. Lisa Marie had never seen a room quite as large before, but it wasn't the room that had stopped her in her tracks. It was what was in the room that had boggled her brain and robbed her of her ability to speak.

Normally, she liked that word. *Boggled.* Right now, though, she couldn't care less about it. Right now, she had more pressing concerns.

"Well, what do you know? I was right," said Bearvis. "This ain't good at all."

15

A teddy bear sat in the ballroom, propped up against the back wall. There was nothing unusual about that—there were dozens of bears in the room. What was unusual was the size of this particular bear.

It was huge.

No. More than that. It was *enormous*.

So massive that, even sitting down, it filled almost the whole room from top to bottom and side to side.

"Behold!" roared Grizz from the doorway. "The Mega-Ted!"

Its fur was a patchwork of different materials, presumably stolen from craft shops and clothes shops all over the city. Some parts were furry; others were made of rough canvas or denim.

"That's a big teddy bear," whispered Vernon.

"*Quack!*" replied Drake, presumably in agreement.

Nine or ten teddies were still working on sewing one of the giant bear's paws together, while several others finished up the face. The bear's eyes were tractor tires, and its nose was a silver oval tray that had been stolen from the palace kitchens.

Down on the floor between the teddy's legs were two complicated-looking machines sitting side by side, each the size of a washing machine. Attached to one were hundreds of little satellite dishes. Lights blinked and flashed in random patterns of color across its front.

Attached to the other by a cable was something that looked like a colander. It had hundreds of wires threaded through the holes in the metal and two old-fashioned lightbulbs fixed to the sides.

"What in tarnation are those things for?" Bearvis wondered.

Lisa Marie had her suspicions but didn't say anything in case she was wrong.

She *really* hoped she was wrong.

There was something else over in the corner. At first, Lisa Marie thought it was some unused fabric meant for the Mega-Ted, but when she looked more closely, she saw that it was a bundle of teddy-sized costumes. Many of them were similar to those the original Halloween bears had worn. She could see witch hats, alien jetpacks, ghostly white tails and more. That wasn't good news. If these bears got dressed up in those outfits, they'd be even harder to stop.

Grizz stood in Ursine's body at the front of the crowd, grinning broadly.

"I brought you here to watch . . . ," Grizz began, then stopped and smirked. "No. Not to watch. To *bear witness* to the single greatest moment in teddy history."

Ursine reached the front and gave the machine with the satellite dishes a stroke, like it was a favorite pet.

"This is the Tedinator. It brought you all to life. It took pieces of my personality and beamed them out to all of you. It created you. *I* created you."

There were a few impressed-sounding *ooh*s at that.

"And soon, once we get it high enough to send the signal, it will spread that same personality to teddy bears around the world," Grizz continued. He tapped himself on the side of the head. "It will take what's in here and transmit it globally. France. Germany. Australia. The United States. All will be affected. Teddy bears will rise up and seize control. All nations will fall. All will be *mine*."

Ursine picked up the colander that was attached to the other machine and placed it on his head. He had quite a big head, so it was a bit of a struggle to get it to fit.

"First, we will make an up-to-date copy of my personality for us to transmit around the world. This way, every new teddy who wakes up will have the plan already in its head," Grizz explained. He nodded to a royal foot-bear, who bowed in reply and then flicked a switch.

Ursine's whole body went stiff and his eyes went wide. He shouted "Potatoes!" very loudly for no apparent reason.

Then the foot-bear flicked the switch again,

pulled a USB stick out of the machine and held it up with both paws, as if proudly showing off a newborn child.

Ursine wiped some drool from his beard, smoothed his shirt, then continued in Grizz's voice.

"We'll stick that into the Tedinator later and beam it into the heads of teddies all over the world," he said, pointing to the machine with the satellite dishes. "But first we'll perform the personality transfer. I'm sick of being stuck inside this meatbag. Time for me to break free."

Lisa Marie's eyes went from Ursine to the giant bear and back again.

"He's going to transfer himself into the Mega-Ted," she whispered.

"He'll be huge," Vernon replied, taking stating the obvious to a whole new level.

"I have a plan," Lisa Marie said. "Listen carefully, and maybe we can—"

She stopped when she realized two Queen's Guard bears were standing beside her. She heard Vernon give a muffled yelp, then turned in time to see two more of the bearskin-wearing teddies grabbing him by the arm.

Up at the front, Ursine's beard split into a toothy grin. "Come on, you really think I didn't see you in there?" he asked. "Look at you. I spotted you towering above the others the moment you walked in."

Lisa Marie and Vernon's masks were pulled off. The bears around them gasped or shrieked in shock.

"They're meatbags!" yelped one.

"Not teddies!" cried another.

"Ew! That's disgusting. I think I'm going to be sick!" wailed a third.

"Quack," said Drake. He hopped out of Vernon's arms and waddled a few paces to his left, hoping no one would realize he was with the children. Unfortunately, it didn't work, and a set of rough paws shoved him back to Vernon's side.

"Aw, what's the matter, girl? Not got your little sequin-wearing friend with you?" Grizz sniggered.

Lisa Marie glanced down at the spot where Bearvis had been standing. The Elvis bear was nowhere to be seen.

"Er, no," she said. "But we don't need him. We'll stop you on our own!"

Ursine's face darkened. "Oh, I don't think so," Grizz replied. "Take them away. Throw them in the dungeon!"

A foot-bear cleared his throat and whispered something.

"What? What do you mean 'no dungeon'? What sort of palace doesn't have a dungeon?"

"This one, Your Majesty," said the foot-bear in a voice like dry autumn leaves. "We have a wine cellar."

Grizz tutted. "Well, that's not the same, is it? 'Throw them in the wine cellar' isn't nearly as scary."

"My apologies, Your Majesty," the foot-bear said. "Would you like us to rename it?"

"Yes," said Grizz. "From now on, it's the dungeon."

"Very good, Your Majesty," the foot-bear said, nodding sharply. He turned and gestured to the guard teddies. "You heard His Majesty. Throw them in the dungeon."

Lisa Marie and Vernon tried to wriggle free as paws grabbed them by the arms and wrestled them toward the door.

"But be careful you don't knock over any of the bottles," the foot-bear called after them. "Those wines cost more than your house!"

16

Vernon ran up the stone steps, threw his full weight at the wine-cellar door, then bounced off and rolled back down the stairs.

"Cut that out!" warned one of the bears that had been posted on guard duty outside the door.

"Ow. That hurt," Vernon muttered from the spot on the floor where he'd landed.

"*Qua-qua-quack!*" laughed Drake.

"It's not funny," Vernon protested, jumping to his feet. He gestured around at the dusty wine cellar. "We're stuck in here. We might never get out! And who knows what they're planning on doing to us? What if they eat us?"

"*Quack,*" said Drake, suddenly finding it less funny.

"No one is eating anyone. They just said that to scare us," said Lisa Marie. She sat on the edge of a small table, looking quite relaxed. "Stop worrying. Everything's fine."

"Fine?!" Vernon yelped. "Fine? How is it fine? Grizz has built a giant body. He has a machine that is going to implant his brain, or whatever, into teddies all over the world, and we're locked in a dungeon!"

"Wine cellar," Lisa Marie corrected him. She got off the table and smoothed down the front of her school uniform. "And yes, most of that stuff is problematic. Except the last part."

"What?" asked Vernon.

"*Quack?*" asked Drake.

"The locked-in-a-wine-cellar part," Lisa Marie said. "It's not a problem."

Vernon frowned. "Why not?"

From the other side of the door, there came two thuds, one after the other. "Hope you fine gentlemen didn't take those karate chops personally," drawled a familiar voice.

Lisa Marie smiled. "That's why not," she said

as the door swung open to reveal Bearvis framed in the doorway.

"Ladies and gentlemen, Bearvis has entered the building," he announced. "But now what do you say we all get outta here?"

"Not yet. First we need to stop Grizz from transferring his personality into the Mega-Ted," Lisa Marie said.

Bearvis winced. "Yeah. About that," he said. "There's a chance we might be too late."

From elsewhere in the palace, there came a thunderous crash that rattled all the wine bottles in their racks. It was the sound of something large punching its way through something solid, and was followed by the roar of hundreds of teddy bears cheering.

"By which I mean, we're *definitely* too late," Bearvis concluded.

"What was that?" Vernon asked.

"It must be the Mega-Ted," Lisa Marie said, hurrying up the cellar steps. "It was too big for the doors. The only way it could liberate itself from the ballroom would be through the wall."

"The only way it could what itself?" asked Vernon, chasing after her.

Lisa Marie sighed. "*Liberate.* It means free itself."

"Well, why didn't you just say that?" Vernon tutted. Now was not the time for big words, he thought. Not unless the word was *Heeeeeeeeeelp!* and he wasn't sure that counted.

They ran up the steps to the wine cellar, heaved open a second wooden door and stumbled into a once-beautiful, now-ruined corridor. The carpet was torn, the windows were broken, and someone had carved TEDIES ROOL into the wall, which upset Lisa Marie on a number of levels, not least because of the spelling.

"Which way to the ballroom?" Lisa Marie asked.

Vernon's eyes went wide. "We're not seriously running *toward* the ballroom, are we? Running *away* from the ballroom would be a much better idea."

"*Quack,*" said Drake, in what was probably agreement.

Bearvis and Lisa Marie ignored them.

"This way, little darlin'," Bearvis announced, powering ahead along the corridor.

They all charged after him as he zipped left around a corner, then almost fell over him when he ground to a halt in the next corridor, his head whipping from side to side as he tried to figure out which direction to go next.

"It's either this way or that way," Bearvis drawled, pointing to the route ahead, then to another corridor that ran off at a right angle. "Or maybe back the way we came."

"This place needs a map," Lisa Marie groaned.

"And an emergency exit," Vernon mumbled. An idea hit him. "Wait! Can't ducks find their way home?"

Lisa Marie, Bearvis and Drake all turned to look at him.

"What?" asked Lisa Marie.

"Ducks," said Vernon, as if that explained everything. When he realized that it didn't, he continued. "Can't they, you know, find their way home? Couldn't Drake find the ballroom for us?"

Lisa Marie smiled. It was a nice smile that said "Well done for trying."

"First of all, he wouldn't be going home. Drake doesn't live in the ballroom of Buckingham Palace."

"*Quack,*" confirmed Drake.

"Well, no, but—"

Lisa Marie cut Vernon off before he could

continue. "And secondly, you're thinking of pigeons. You get homing pigeons. Not homing ducks."

She turned on her heels and regarded both corridors ahead. "Now, if I were a royal ballroom, where would I be hiding?"

Vernon pointed down one of the corridors. "That way."

Lisa Marie squinted along the passageway. "I'm not sure," she said after a moment.

"It is. It's that way," Vernon insisted. "Trust me."

"Says the guy who invented the homing duck," Bearvis said. He pointed down the other corridor. "You ask me? I reckon it's this a-way."

"Well, you're wrong," said Vernon, crossing his arms. "It's that way."

Lisa Marie frowned. "How can you be so sure?"

"I just know these things," said Vernon.

"*Quack.*"

Vernon sighed and shot Drake a dirty look. Then he jabbed a thumb over his shoulder. "There's a sign on the wall with an arrow on it pointing the way."

"Well, all right, then," Bearvis said. "I guess I stand corrected."

Three of them set off running again, and one broke into a fast waddle, heading for the palace ballroom.

Or what was left of it.

17

The first thing everyone noticed about the ballroom was that the ceiling and much of one wall were missing. Rubble had rained down onto the polished wooden floor, and one of the grand chandeliers was now nothing more than shards of broken crystal.

The second thing they noticed was a distinct lack of teddy bears. The giant bear had gone, but so had all the others, taking the Tedinator with them. The machine Grizz had used to make a backup of his personality was still there. Lisa Marie made a mental note of that before glancing at the corner where she'd seen the pile of costumes earlier. She was dismayed to find them gone too.

The third thing they noticed was Ursine Kodiak. The man was hanging upside down from the one remaining chandelier, his feet tied together with a length of rope, his face bright red from all the blood rushing to his head.

He hung limply, both arms dangling toward the floor, his beard flopping down so it almost covered his face.

"Children! Oh, thank goodness!" he cried. "Something terrible has happened to me."

"Something terrible has happened to the whole country," Lisa Marie snapped. "And it's all your fault!"

Ursine smiled nervously, but no one could see it through the beard. "Ha ha. Yes. Quite. In my defense, I was under Grizz's control, so I can't really be blamed for—"

"We don't care," said Lisa Marie. "Just tell us where Grizz is going."

"You can't stop him," Ursine whispered. "He can't be beaten. There's nothing you can do. But I have an underground bunker. I could take you there. We could all hide and be safe. And maybe in, say, twenty years, things might have settled down."

Lisa Marie crossed her arms and shot her sternest look up at Ursine. "I'm going to ask you one more time," she said firmly. "Where is he going?"

"I suggest you answer her, son," said Bearvis. "You do not want to make her angry."

"I—I don't know where he's going," Ursine admitted. "He said something about having to get high up. He's going to use the Tedinator to bring teddies to life all over the world."

"How high would he have to be for the signal to reach the whole world?" Lisa Marie asked.

"Not *very* high, I suppose," said Ursine. He did some quick working-out in his head, which wasn't easy, as his upside-down brain felt like it was going to explode. "Three hundred yards or so should do it."

Lisa Marie nodded and turned back to the door. "I know where he's going. Come on!"

"Wait, don't leave me!" Ursine protested. "Get me down."

"No chance. You're staying right where you are," Vernon told him.

"*Quack,*" agreed Drake.

They both hurried to keep up with Lisa Marie and Bearvis as they made for the door.

"Where are we going? Do we have a plan?" Vernon asked.

"Not yet," Lisa Marie admitted.

"What?" Vernon yelped, stumbling to a stop. "You *always* have a plan!"

Lisa Marie stopped too. She turned to him, a worried expression on her face. "Not this time, Vernon," she said. "There are so many of them, and he's so big, and I have no idea how to—"

She fell silent and froze, as if her batteries had run out. Vernon waved a hand in front of her face, then followed her gaze. She was looking past him at something on the other side of the ballroom.

The machine. The machine with the colander

helmet. The machine Grizz had used to make a copy of his personality.

Suddenly she jumped back to life.

"Sorry, I was thinking," she said. "And I take it back."

"Take what back?" Vernon asked.

Lisa Marie smiled. "I *do* have a plan."

She spun around to face Bearvis and Drake. "And I'm going to need your help."

Twenty minutes later, following some fast driving from Bearvis, a lot of screaming from Vernon, and a series of panicky quacks from Drake, they all jumped out of a long black limousine they'd "borrowed" from the palace garage and raced toward a towering glass building.

"Are you sure this is where he'll go?" Vernon asked.

"I'm sure," said Lisa Marie. "The Shard is the

tallest building in London. At over a thousand feet, it's the perfect height." She pointed up. "Also, he's right there."

Vernon, Drake and Bearvis all followed her finger. Moonlight reflected off the mirrored glass of the Shard, except for a darkened bear-shaped area, where no light was getting through. It was moving slowly up the side of the building, the Tedinator clutched in one hand.

Squinting, Vernon tried to study the figure more closely, but it was already too high and almost lost in the darkness.

"Are we sure that's him?"

Bearvis frowned. "Well, unless there's some other giant teddy bear getting up to no good around these parts, I reckon it's a safe bet, son."

Vernon surveyed the empty street. "Where are the other bears?"

There was movement from over on their left.

Lisa Marie tutted. "Oh, you had to ask, didn't you?" she said.

Three bears leaped out from behind an abandoned car. One was dressed like a Viking and

carried a double-headed battle-axe. Another was dressed like an evil space warrior, complete with cape, black mask and a breathing device that made a loud wheezing sound every couple of seconds.

The third bear had painted his face white, and wore a stripy black-and-white sweater. His paws were positioned in a way that suggested he was holding a sword, but Lisa Marie couldn't actually see one.

It took her a second to figure out what the costume was supposed to be. Once she did, she groaned. "Ugh. He's a mime."

"Well, that doesn't sound very dangerous," said Vernon.

The mime bear swung with his invisible sword. There was a loud *chink* and part of the car the bears had been hiding behind fell off and clattered to the ground.

Vernon gulped. "Er, I take that back," he said.

The Viking twirled his axe.

The mime waved his invisible blade.

And then, with an electrical buzz, the space-warrior bear activated a laser sword, and a short beam of red light shot out from a handle he clutched in his paws.

"That's actually pretty awesome," Vernon whispered.

"Quack," agreed Drake.

Lisa Marie peered up at the Shard. Grizz was over halfway to the top now, barely visible in the gloom. They were running out of time.

"We have to get up there and stop him," Lisa Marie said, then ducked as something came swooshing by her, narrowly missing her head.

A witch bear cackled as she streaked past on her broom. And she wasn't alone. Lisa Marie, Vernon, Bearvis and the duck all bunched together as they saw a small army of teddy bears come creeping from the shadows.

There were vampires, werewolves, ghosts and goblins. Lisa Marie saw bears dressed as sharks, octopuses, dinosaurs and all sorts of other scary creatures. They growled and showed off their sharp teeth. Especially the sharks and dinosaurs, who had a *lot* of teeth to show off.

"You three, go put the plan into action," said

Bearvis. "I'll stay here and hold these guys back."

He ran a paw through his hair, adopted a karate stance and curled his lip into a sneer. "Now, come on, you ugly mommas," he said, beckoning to the evil teddies. "Let me show you what the *real* King can do!"

Lisa Marie, Vernon and Drake hurried through the doors of the Shard and raced past reception desks and expensive-looking couches until they came to a door marked STAIRS.

"You have got to be kidding me!" said Vernon. "We can't take the stairs!"

"The power's out," Lisa Marie said. "We don't have any choice."

"It's a million stories high!" Vernon pointed out.

"It's actually ninety-five stories," said Lisa Marie. "Although the seventy-second is the highest habitable floor. It's actually a really interesting structure with—"

The *haaawp* of a breathing apparatus and the

bzzz of a laser sword activating behind them cut Lisa Marie off. A red glow illuminated the door to the stairs.

"I've been waiting for you, meatbags," said a space-warrior bear. This teddy was taller than the space warrior outside, and looked even more menacing.

A jetpack on his back ignited, launching him a few yards across the hallway and dropping him closer to Lisa Marie, Vernon and Drake. The bear twirled his sword, the beam humming as it sliced through the air. "Now, witness my power, and the power of the Dark Si—"

The teddy stopped as he misjudged the spin and the laser sword sliced off one of his own arms.

He stared at the arm lying on the floor for a while, then winced behind his mask. "*Ooh*, that's not good," he muttered.

He lowered the sword, but was so distracted by his missing arm that he didn't notice he had chopped off his own leg until it was too late. He toppled sideways and fell to the floor, his laser sword rolling out of reach.

"I'll take that!" said Vernon, pouncing on the sword and snatching it up. He grinned as he swished it through the air. "This is *amazing!*"

"*Quack!*" protested Drake, dodging out of the sword's path.

"Be careful!" said Lisa Marie.

"Give that back," the fallen teddy protested, but no one was listening to him.

Lisa Marie looked at the sword in Vernon's hand. She looked at the fallen bear, his stuffing spilling from his self-inflicted wounds.

And then she looked at the jetpack strapped to his back.

"No," she said out loud. "No. That's crazy."

Vernon stopped swooshing the sword for a minute and frowned at her. "What's crazy?"

Lisa Marie smiled sheepishly. "What would you say if I told you we didn't have to take the stairs?"

Vernon's face lit up with excitement. "I'd say that's *great!*"

Lisa Marie shrugged. "Okay. Then let's do it."

"Not great! Not great!" Vernon screamed. "I've changed my mind! I want to take the stairs!"

It was too late for that, though. Vernon clung tightly to Lisa Marie as she rocketed up the side of the Shard, her borrowed jetpack spewing blue fire behind her. Drake was squashed between them, his eyes screwed tightly shut as they rose higher and higher.

They had made it a third of the way up before anyone below had spotted them. Several more jetpack-wearing teddies, a handful of witches and at least one fairy were now giving chase.

Lisa Marie tried not to think about the bears below them and concentrated on the bear above. She narrowed her eyes against the oncoming wind and squinted up at the top of the building.

Grizz was now at the very top, holding on to the side with one hand while he placed the Tedinator in position with the other. This was going to be close!

Lisa Marie cranked the control dial of the jetpack all the way up to full power. Vernon squealed and Drake honked as they streaked upward, leaving the ground far, far below.

They were thirty floors up now. Forty. Fifty. Each story passed in a flash. Even over the rushing of the wind, Lisa Marie could hear Grizz laughing to himself, cackling about the victory he was about to win.

Lisa Marie gritted her teeth as they sped up-ward. Grizz wouldn't win if she had anything to do with it!

"Okay, does everyone remember the plan?" she asked.

Vernon squeaked. "I don't remember my own name right now!"

"*Quack*," agreed Drake.

"Pull yourselves together," Lisa Marie scolded. "We've got one chance to save the world. We can't blow it. We *won't*."

Vernon swallowed, but then nodded. "Okay," he said. "L-let's do it."

Lisa Marie nodded to him. "Keep him busy."

Vernon shoved two fingers in his mouth, took a deep breath, then whistled.

Well, he tried to whistle, but what came out was a sort of *bleeurf* noise and a lot of saliva.

"Sorry—nerves," he explained. Then he tried again. This time, it worked.

Pheeewe-pheeep!

Overhead, Grizz looked down just as a high-speed ball of boy, girl and duck rocketed up. He swung out from the side of the building, holding on with one hand, avoiding the impact.

"Missed!" cried Vernon.

"I noticed," said Lisa Marie, grimacing.

They overshot the top of the Shard, looped in the air, then swung around for another attack. The Tedinator was already in place, although it hadn't yet been switched on. There was still time.

The Mega-Ted's enormous paw swatted at them, forcing Lisa Marie to bank sharply out of its path. The children and the duck saw themselves reflected in one of the Shard's mirrored windows before Lisa Marie pulled away and circled around once more.

"You meatbags again!" Grizz snarled. "I should've known! You just can't leave me alone, can you?"

"Not a chance," Lisa Marie said. She buzzed close to Grizz's head, forcing him to duck out of the way, then turned and shot toward the Tedinator.

They had almost reached it when one of Grizz's giant paws clipped their jetpack, sending them all into a frantic, out-of-control spin.

"Hold on!" Lisa Marie yelped.

"I'm going to throw up!" Vernon cried.

"Quack-qua-quacking-quack!" protested Drake, who was directly in Vernon's vomit path.

Lisa Marie managed to get the jetpack under control just as the alien bears and witches arrived on the scene. Energy blasts came screaming toward the children from several Zap-o-Matic Death Rays.

Shoom. The laser sword activated in Vernon's hand. He swung wildly with it, deflecting most of the energy blasts and sending them back the way they'd come.

Three aliens crashed as they tried to dodge the beams. They shook their fists as they plunged down the side of the building and collided with the fairy, who was still fluttering several floors below.

"Nice work!" Lisa Marie said.

Vernon smiled shakily. "Th-thanks. I used to have a plastic one. I was pretty good with it, but this one's much cooler."

He gave the laser sword a twirl, then gasped

as it slipped from his fingers and went plunging toward the ground far below.

Vernon smiled nervously at his stepsister. "I said I was *pretty* good with it. I didn't say I was an expert."

Lisa Marie rocketed them around the side of the building, trying to shake off a couple of witches who were screeching after them.

"We have to get to the Tedinator before Grizz can activate it," Lisa Marie said.

One of Grizz's massive paws swiped at them

again. Lisa Marie dodged it, but a passing witch wasn't so lucky. She hissed angrily as she fell off her broom and tumbled down the side of the Shard.

The broom, free of its rider, sped up. It was about to zoom past the children when Lisa Marie grabbed it.

"Here, take this," she told Vernon.

Confused, he reached out and took hold of the broom. "What now?" he asked.

"Hold on," Lisa Marie instructed. She tucked Drake under one arm, put her other hand on Vernon's chest and pushed.

Vernon screamed as he swung away from his stepsister. For a split second, he was falling, but then the broom kicked in and began dragging him through the air.

"What are you doing?!" Vernon screeched.

"We're going to take out the Tedinator," Lisa Marie called to him. "You keep the witches busy."

"How am I supposed to do that?" Vernon cried back.

"No idea," Lisa Marie admitted. "Think of something."

Before Vernon could answer, she adjusted the controls of the jetpack and climbed steeply, twisting and spinning to avoid another of Grizz's swipes.

"You ready for this, Drake?" she asked,

steering them toward the open-air viewing deck right at the top of the Shard.

"*Quack*," said Drake.

"I have no idea what you just said," Lisa Marie told him. "But I'm going to take it as a yes."

19

Lisa Marie and Drake landed clumsily on the viewing platform, bounced once on the floor, then clattered to a stop against a staircase railing.

They both jumped up in time to see Vernon streaking past the outside of the building, two witches in hot pursuit, flinging fireballs at him from their wands.

"Heeeeeeelp!" he bellowed.

"You're doing great!" Lisa Marie cheered. "Just one more minute and we'll—"

"And you'll *what*?" boomed Grizz, his head appearing above the Shard's pointed top. "What are you even doing here, meatbag? You can't stop me. Nothing can stop me!"

"Want to bet?" cried Lisa Marie. "Drake, now!"

172

Drake broke into a running waddle and extended his wings. He lurched awkwardly into the air, flapping at Grizz's face.

Meanwhile, Lisa Marie set off running toward the Tedinator. It was fixed to the outside of the building, but she could reach it if she leaned out far enough. She just had to hope Drake kept Grizz busy long enough for her to get to it.

Quaaaack!

Drake crashed to the floor beside her in a cloud of feathers. A piece of plastic almost fell out of his beak, but he snapped it shut just in time.

"Nice try!" Grizz snarled. "But it's going to take more than a duck to distract me."

A paw that was bigger than her whole body shoved Lisa Marie backward. She stumbled and fell, landing on her bottom with a *thump* that made Grizz snigger gleefully.

Lisa Marie sniffed and wiped her eyes on the sleeve of her school sweater.

"Aw, the meatbag is crying," said Grizz. His tractor-tire eyes seemed to light up with delight. "Such a shame. Poor little girl."

"I'm not crying," Lisa Marie replied, wiping her eyes and choking back a sob.

"You're *totally* crying," cackled Grizz. Behind him, Vernon went spinning past on the broom, the witches still hot on his tail.

Lisa Marie stood up and cleared her throat. "I'm not crying!" she insisted.

It was only then that Grizz saw the smile on her face.

"I'm distracting you," she said.

Grizz's patchwork forehead furrowed into a frown. He looked down to see Drake fluttering out from inside the Tedinator, looking quite smug for a duck.

"Drake, did you do it?" Lisa Marie yelled.

A paw flicked the duck off the machine before he could quack a reply. Drake flapped his wings in the air for a few moments, trying to get back to the Tedinator, but he wasn't used to flying and quickly crashed back down onto the viewing platform.

"Nice try, meatbag," Grizz said. "You almost got me. But this time, I win. You hear me? *I win!*"

He prodded the Tedinator. Lights illuminated all over its surface. Lisa Marie could only watch as the satellite dishes moved into position, preparing to beam out the signal.

"Yes!" Grizz cheered. "YES!"

A screen unfolded from inside the machine.

"Show me!" Grizz commanded, and the screen

illuminated to show several different images, all coming from different cameras around the world. They seemed to be live feeds from toy shops, and all showed several motionless, glassy-eyed bears.

The Tedinator hummed. Grizz cackled with delight. "Watch, meatbag!" he said, indicating the screen. "Watch me take over the whole wide world!"

At first, nothing happened. Then, in one of the images down at the bottom left, a paw twitched.

"It's working!" Grizz bellowed. "It's working!"

Sure enough, bears had started to come to life in all of the images now. Lisa Marie read the names of the countries in each picture: Japan. France. Poland. Canada. The signal had already reached the far corners of the earth, bringing bears to life everywhere.

"I did it!" Grizz cried. "I did it! My personality has infected teddy bears all over the planet. The world is mine! It's finally—"

"Aw, man, I came to life," said a voice from the screen. It was a familiar voice, with a distinctive deep Southern accent. One of the teddies was patting its head. "Hey, where's my hair, man? Where's the King's beautiful hair?"

Grizz's face took on a look of confusion. "What? Why's he saying that?"

More voices emerged from the speakers, all sounding similar to the first one. "Hey there. Anyone know what's going on?"

"Afraid not, son. The King's just as clueless as you are."

"Well, I appreciate you taking the time to

JAPAN FRANCE

POLAND CANAD

INDIA CHINA

answer, buddy," another voice said. "Thank you. Thank you very much."

Grizz's tractor-tire eyes widened. He peered down at the machine, and the USB stick wedged into the slot. It was a different color than the one he'd stored his personality on.

"Looking for this?" asked Lisa Marie, taking the original USB stick from Drake's beak. She dropped it on the floor, then stamped it under her heel.

"NO!" Grizz bellowed.

"Yes," said Lisa Marie, smiling sweetly. "We weren't here to stop the Tedinator, just to stop your personality from being transmitted. Drake swapped the USB sticks when you had your back turned."

Drake quacked proudly.

"You just beamed Bearvis's personality to every teddy bear in the world," Lisa Marie explained. She leaned in closer and smiled. "And Bearvis *really* doesn't like you."

Two witch bears appeared in the air beside

him. They stood on their brooms in karate poses, their top lips curling into snarls. "And she means *every* teddy bear, son," one of the witches drawled, sounding exactly like Bearvis. She looked across to the other witch. "What say we take care of business?"

"Uh-huh-huh," said the second witch, wriggling her hips. They both opened fire with their wands, and two fireballs struck Grizz on the forehead. He hissed and fell backward, his grip slipping from the side of the building.

"Noooo!" he cried as he began to tumble. There was a *rrrrrip* as his stitched-together belly caught on the corner of an open window.

As Grizz fell, he began to unravel. His body fell apart in long strips of fur, leather and denim, spilling enormous rolls of stuffing out into the air, where it was carried off by the wind.

Lisa Marie and Drake rushed to the edge of the viewing platform to watch as what remained of Grizz plunged down, down, down into the darkness.

"It's over," Lisa Marie said, sagging against the railing. "We did it! It's all over."

Vernon shot past on his broom, screaming at the top of his voice.

"*Quack,*" said Drake.

Lisa Marie nodded and giggled. "Okay, we'll get Vernon down, and *then* it'll be all over."

Ten minutes later, with the help of the witches, Lisa Marie, Vernon and Drake the duck touched down on the pavement outside the Shard. The battle that had been raging there was over. The bears that had been fighting now cheered, waved and made complimentary remarks about each other's hairstyles.

"Well, I guess the plan worked out just fine!" said Bearvis, rushing over to them. "One minute,

they're all trying to kill me, the next thing I know, they're all trying to be me."

Lisa Marie smiled at him. "You should probably get used to it. They're not the only ones."

Vernon laughed. "Well, you did it again, Lisa Marie," he said.

"We all did it," Lisa Marie corrected him. She looked around at the teddy bears. There would be no way Agent Strong could hide all this lot. She had no idea what would happen, but she had a feeling that the world was going to be a very different place from now on.

A much furrier, cuddlier place.

"Ah well, looks like that's another adventure over," Lisa Marie said. She linked arms with her stepbrother and started strolling toward the limousine. "Nothing else to do."

"*Quack.*"

"Yep," agreed Vernon. "All loose ends tied up. Nothing more to be done."

"*Quack!*"

"You can say that again," said Bearvis. "Show's over."

Drake waddled after them. *"Quack-qua-quack!"*

Lisa Marie stopped and turned around. She held up a tiny witch's wand. "Just kidding, Drake. Of course we're going to change you back."

"Quaaack," said Drake, relieved.

Lisa Marie smirked and slipped the wand back into her pocket. "Eventually," she said.

There was a sudden screech as a pizza van skidded to a halt beside them. Agent Strong jumped out, his fists raised. His suit was torn, and one of the lenses had popped out of his sunglasses.

"Finally took care of those teddies back at the facility," he wheezed. "Now I'm here to help. Let's go stop the bad guys."

"Too late," said Vernon.

"Quack," agreed Drake.

"You missed all the excitement, son," said Bearvis. "Lisa Marie took care of business."

"We *all* took care of business," Lisa Marie corrected him.

"Oh," said Agent Strong. He blinked several times and looked around at the assembled army of teddy bears. They were all adopting karate poses, shaking their hips and laughing. "But . . . the bears. There are still bears."

"I don't think they'll cause too many problems now," said Lisa Marie. She and the others clambered into the royal limousine, with Drake scrabbling in behind.

Agent Strong continued to stare at the bears in confusion as Bearvis fired up the engine. The headlights shone like spotlights on the bears ahead of him. Instinctively, they began to dance and sing, their voices rising like a chorus through the darkened streets of London.

"A little less hibernation, a little more action . . ."

"Aw, man, this is gonna take some getting used to," Bearvis said.

Lisa Marie hugged him. "Long live the King," she said.

Bearvis hugged her back. "Thank you, little darlin'," he told her. "Thank you very much."

EPILOGUE

The next day, many miles outside London, an old woman sat on her front porch, enjoying the fresh autumn breeze. She clutched a knitting needle in each wrinkled hand, the points clicking together as she knitted a brightly colored garment.

The woman hummed quietly to herself as she worked, occasionally glancing up to admire the bright crisp morning, with its blue skies and fluffy white clouds.

As she looked, one of the clouds seemed to break away from the others. Her needles stopped moving as she watched the cloud come drifting toward her. It was only when it thwapped her in the face that she realized it wasn't a cloud at all.

It was a strand of white stuffing.

"Where did you come from?" she wondered, setting down her knitting and turning the stuffing over in her hands. There was quite a lot of it. Just enough, she thought.

"That's handy," she said, folding the stuffing into a neat rectangle. For a moment, she thought she felt it wriggle in her hands, as if it were alive, but she quickly dismissed it as just her imagination.

She leaned forward in her chair and felt beneath the table for her knitting bag. She already had all the wool she needed, and now she had the stuffing too.

"Must be my lucky day," she said, and placed the stuffing in the bag next to the yarn.

That done, she sat up straight, picked up her knitting needles again and peered over her glasses at the knitting pattern on the table beside her. The instructions were laid out neatly on the left-hand page.

On the right-hand page was a photograph of the thing she was knitting. Its glassy eyes gazed out at her from its smiling furry face.

"My grandson is going to just *love* you," she whispered.

And then, with the stuffing squirming in her knitting bag, she set to work.

READ THEM ALL!

ABOUT THE AUTHOR

Barry Hutchison was born and raised in the Highlands of Scotland. He was just eight years old when he decided he wanted to become a writer and seventeen when he sold his first piece of work. In addition to the Night of the Living Ted series, he is the author of the Invisible Fiends series and *The Shark-Headed Bear Thing*. He also writes for TV. Barry lives in Fort William, Scotland, with his partner and their two children.

ABOUT THE ILLUSTRATOR

Lee Cosgrove has been doodling for as long as he can remember. He doodled in his schoolbooks and now he is doodling in children's books. He's probably doodling right now while you're reading this! Lee lives with his wife and two children in Cheshire, England.